MARTIN RU

Cens

COLLINS, 8 GRAFTON STREET, LONDON W1

William Collins Sons & Co. Ltd
London · Glasgow · Sydney · Auckland
Toronto · Johannesburg

First published 1984
© Martin Russell 1984

British Library Cataloguing in Publication Data

Russell, Martin
  Censor.—(Crime Club)
  I. Title
  823′.914[F]   PR6068.U86

  ISBN 0 00 231948 9

Photoset in Linotron Baskerville by
Rowland Phototypesetting Ltd
Bury St Edmunds, Suffolk
Printed in Great Britain by
William Collins Sons & Co. Ltd, Glasgow

CHAPTER 1

News of the violent death of Sir John Wallington came through in good time to catch the later editions, which was in accordance with the courtesy he had always extended to Fleet Street. Sir John, screen thriller director of the decade, had had the additional thoughtfulness to provide his own scenario. It was midnight when he had walked away from the studded doors of the First Reel Club, off Piccadilly, declined the offer of a taxi from the doorman and set off, alone, at a brisk pace in the direction of The Mall via St James's, averring that the exercise would help to reduce the cranial inflation induced by the many kind things that had been said about him by idolizing colleagues since the conclusion of dinner. In a sense, he was right.

An hour later, said the despatch from our crime man, Gil Purvis, the body of the venerable director was found by a young French couple, in London on vacation, behind bushes near the lake in St James's Park. His head injuries were described by police as the work of a maniac. They were hunting, they said, 'a very dangerous criminal indeed—a psychopath with a lust for destruction'. Citizens were advised to avoid the area at night, or proceed in groups.

Much of Purvis's hastily cobbled half-column was up-holstered with detail of Sir John's career, from his storming of the cinema as the doomed avenger in the classic chiller *Night and the Mallards*, circa 1946, to his ultimate achievement as director of three award-winning horror movies in the space of the past two years, culminating in a knighthood which was generally agreed to be as richly merited as it was overdue. A professional associate (reported Purvis, without specifying which one) commented: 'How ghastly that he should go like this, a victim of just the sort of mindless violence which he exploited with such skill and insight in his screen work. John was at the peak of his powers. He will be irreplaceable.'

'*Avoid the area at night,*' scoffed my younger daughter, Elaine, over her morning muesli and apple juice. 'Does that mean we can draw a dotted line around the park and stroll outside it in perfect safety? Who are the police trying to fool?'

'They have to contribute something,' I said, 'on these occasions.'

'I suppose newspaper editors get the same urge. Write a blistering Comment, Dad.'

'Surely you read my piece last Tuesday?'

'*The Case for Vigilantes,*' she quoted, to my surprise. 'I did spot the headline, only Jimmy called before I could . . . What did it say?'

'There's a back-number over there.'

'No time now. Let's see if I can guess. In view of the admitted difficulties facing the police, the argument for quasi-official civilian patrols on the streets of Britain's major cities can no longer be ignored by those who . . . etcetera, etcetera . . . passed to you, Commissioner, and your good chum the Home Secretary, with best wishes and a couple of derisory snorts from your ever-watchful friend and counsellor, the *Planet*. Remember, next time it could be the Chancellor's frail old mum herself. This juice,' concluded Elaine, 'is starting to ferment.'

'You did read it,' I said accusingly.

'No, honestly. But I have known you now for a good few years.'

'I hope I'm not boring you.'

She sent a pert smile across her plate. 'Likewise. Seriously though, Dad—what about yourself? You're always arriving home in the small hours. What precautions do you take?'

'I wear a suit of armour. It's called a Cavalier 1600 GL.'

'But you have to walk to and from the car. Who knows about it? How often do you—'

'My dear, if we're going to have a defence review, let's all come under scrutiny. What time, for example, does this current production of yours finish? Eleven? So it's getting on for midnight when you travel home from a fairly seedy neighbourhood. Had you thought about that?'

'Jimmy looks after me,' she said complacently, exchanging coffee for the apple juice.

'Is he always going to be available? I thought he was directing something at The Backstage shortly.'

'That's right.' Elaine continued to look pleased with herself. 'And guess who he'll be bossing about?'

'You've landed a part?'

'*The* part. It's a brace of new one-acters by Rick Smythe. Different characters in each except for the female lead, who provides the link. That's me.'

'Marvellous.' I blew her a kiss. The news explained why she looked even more radiant than usual, why her coppery hair had an extra sheen to it and her emerald eyes were sending out a sparkle that fell like sunlit rain over the breakfast table. At the age of twenty, my younger daughter had yet to outgrow a child's rapture at good fortune. 'I'm delighted,' I told her, in case she was in any doubt. 'How long is it scheduled to run?'

'Oh, The Backstage, bless it, never puts up with anything for more than three weeks. But it does pull in the Press scouts, and should they happen to like what they see . . .' She drew a breath. 'Well, after all, *Magic Circle* transferred from there to the West End just a few months ago. You never know your luck.'

I smiled. 'I'll see that our drama section gets the message.'

'Don't make a big thing of it,' she said anxiously.

'I'll be discreet. Can't have any whiff of nepotism creeping into the *Planet*'s atmosphere.'

'I'd hate it. Don't think I'm not grateful . . .'

'I won't. What are they like, these new Smythe offerings?'

'I get raped twice and I have an affair with my half-sister, but it's Art.'

'Much nudity?'

'Down to my pants, most of the time,' she said absently, scanning a letter she had just ripped from its envelope. 'That's during the sedate moments, of course. In the steamier scenes—'

'Okay, I think I get the picture.'

Elaine glanced up. 'It's not as decadent as it might sound. There really is an underlying message. If there wasn't, I wouldn't have agreed to do it, you know that.'

'Of course I do,' I said lightly. 'You're not your mother's girl for nothing.'

Leaving her frowning at the notepaper, I went over to the open-plan kitchen area and made myself tea and toast. On my return with the tray, Elaine looked up again. 'I'd have done that for you. I got absorbed in this rather odd fan-letter. That is, I think it's from a fan. I've been trying to puzzle it out.'

'What's odd about it?'

'The wording, I suppose. He or she—I can't decipher the signature—doesn't say the usual things: loved your perform-ance, worthy of a better vehicle, best of luck in the future, blah blah. This one—' she peered down at the sheet—'just says, "Dear Miss Rodgers, you don't belong on the top floor of The Peacock, you should have both feet planted firmly at ground-floor stage level to fulfil your undoubted talents. Sincerely, Squiggle.'''

'That's all?'

'In its entirety. Nice, huh? I think.'

'It seems to be intended as a compliment. Was it delivered here?'

'No, I was given it last night, as I left.'

I inspected the envelope. 'Just your name typed on it—no stamp or postmark. Must have been dropped in by hand.'

'I don't care,' Elaine said dreamily, 'how they reach me. They all go into the dossier. My personal insurance against menopausal depression.' Skating the note accurately on to the top of the dresser, she returned to a businesslike stance. 'Getting back to offstage violence . . . you will watch out for yourself, Dad, until this latest maniac is under lock and key? Promise? You're a night bird, after all. You have to be—'

'Don't fret, darling.' I patted her wrist. 'Between Planet House and here, the only fresh air I sniff is from the car's ventilation. Any attacker would need to be Superman to get at me.'

She studied me dubiously. 'That's probably what Sir John Wallington would have said, if he'd given it a thought.'

CHAPTER 2

That day's first editorial conference was a more than usually taxing event.

Dave Windsor, our chief diplomatic correspondent, was in argumentative mood over revelations he wanted to publish about British embassies in the Third World; as a result, the row that had been seething for several days between him and the features editor, who craved space for the serialization of some spicy diary entries by the aristocratic wife of a property developer of national repute, came abruptly to the boil. A soccer scandal was jostling for position on the news pages. The pictures editor had new, provocative shots of the latest and tiniest in fashion beachwear, which clamoured for a centre-spread; and there were stories of vice and corruption in three separate town halls which demanded at least a full page to themselves, plus another for the interesting background. The slaughter of Sir John Wallington at a moment of triumph could hardly be overlooked, and to cap it all, because of an unexpected drop in advertising volume, we were restricted for the next few days to smaller than normal editions. None of this was anything new, but it had come at an awkward time.

'Something,' I pronounced, 'will have to go.'

'Embassies,' the features editor said promptly. 'Who's interested in 'em?'

'Ambassadors,' someone remarked.

'Surely it's our job,' Dave Windsor retorted tetchily, 'to *make* people interested. It's their money that's being used.'

'Our job is to sell copies.'

'Misuse of Government funds is still a selling-point.'

'So is flesh. Right, Peter?' said the pictures editor, appealing to me. 'Nobody buys the *Planet* under the delusion that it's a Government White Paper, do they? People get it off bookstands, not HMSO.'

'I wasn't suggesting otherwise,' breathed Windsor, with iron restraint. 'My contention is, in the midst of half a dozen pages given over to the bedroom antics of assorted public servants and landed gentry, we could surely—'

It was time to intervene. 'I take both points,' I said soothingly, 'and I'd love to be all things to all readers, but sadly we've the customary quarts and pints problem, so we need to reach some kind of a decision now.' I glanced at the clock. 'Look, Dave, how about a compromise? I know you've sweated blood on the embassies story, and I agree it's important to the taxpayers. Can we hold it until next week, then pin it to the public expenditure rumpus that's coming up?'

'So that it becomes just another statistic, buried on page two?'

His annoyance infected me. 'We do take things a mite

seriously, now and then. The actual treatment is for Wally and me to decide.'

'By this time next week, nine more sex scandals will have made the decision for you.'

Noting the smiles on the lips of the others, I swallowed my wrath and humoured him. 'Okay, so we direct most of our energies along certain channels . . . who's arguing? Our sales figure says all that's necessary. Without it, you and I could be out of a job. But let me assure you, Dave—there's still a place for crusading journalism on the *Planet*. Your turn will come.' As an extra emollient, I added, 'Meanwhile, we're using your piece on Lord Bell, which I like very much.'

'I'm flattered.' He didn't sound it.

Gil Purvis spoke up. 'How about Wallington? Is he going to be dead by tomorrow? If you'll forgive the expression.'

'Depends what you've dug up. Anything?'

'Not in the way you mean. His personal life seems to have been purity itself.'

'I find that a little hard to believe. Not married, was he?'

'No, but from what I hear you can forget about that. He lived with an older sister in a mansion block near Victoria Station. Quiet social life, a few close friends of the respectable variety, no known excesses, no offbeat propensities . . . zero. Just a steadfast dedication to his work, one damn film after another. Sorry, Peter. I did try.'

'I don't doubt it.' I weighed the question. 'So, we ditch the follow-up?'

Purvis shrugged. 'Unless there's a breakthrough on the murder weapon, or his sister confesses to the crime.'

'Okay. We'll carry a couple of the less nauseating tributes from showbiz, and you might do a speculative piece—was he watched when leaving the club? did someone simply leap out of the bushes?—in case it's needed. After the initial sensation, I can't see many people working up a lather over the death of a seventy-year-old film director, eminent or not. It was probably a straight mugging. I'll bear it in mind for my next Comment on street safety.'

Subdued guffaws shook the room. 'No lack of raw material,' observed the features editor. 'Leaving Wallington aside, in the past month or two we've had Paul Lewis, the scriptwriter, and . . . who was that TV guy?'

'Carl Scott?'

'That's it, the series mogul. Come to think of it, he copped it at home, in his study. But it was another violent end, for all that. As for Lewis . . . On the footway, fifty yards from his house, wasn't it? Not a blunt instrument, though, as I recall.'

'No. A knife of some kind.'

'Anyhow it left him just as dead.' The features editor looked gnomishly around. 'Are we through?'

There was a general move towards departure. As the last of them filed out I activated the intercom. 'Anyone there yet from Drama?'

Dave Windsor, the last in line, paused to throw me a cynical look before following the rest outside and shutting the door.

'Kershaw,' said a tired voice.

''Morning, Ron. Sounds as if you had a late sitting at the Criterion. Look, I just thought I'd mention this. It appears that Rick Smythe, the White Hope of the British theatre, has a new two-parter coming along at the—'

'We know about it,' he said on a note of additional fatigue. 'A three-week run at The Backstage. Two acts with a split down the middle, or some such nonsense. Why?'

'A note reached me about it,' I lied, 'so I thought I should pass on the information.' He said nothing. There was no help for it. 'To be honest, Ron, my daughter has the lead role in the production.'

'Good for her.' He said it calmly. 'We'll send someone along.'

'Only if you've a body spare.'

'We'll cope.' A quiet laugh pursued the remark. I thought it politic to send one back, so I did.

'If you feel I'm twisting your arm, old son, it's because I am. In a subtle way, she twisted mine first.'

'Can't say I blame her. Why pass up a useful connection? Leaving that aside,' added Ron Kershaw, who was not noted for sycophancy, 'she's very good. I saw her a little while back, in *Stew Pot*. Highly promising.'

'I'd like to tell her that, only I won't. Thanks, Ron, I'm grateful. But don't feel under an obligation.'

'As if I would.'

If there was irony in the retort, he masked it well. Switching off, I stood up, wandered to the window. Supported by the sill, I gazed down at the tops of vehicles as they struggled along the near-stagnant canal of Fleet Street, five storeys below. Although I had work to do, I held this position for some while.

String-pulling repelled me. Its crude effectiveness was something I had always classified as degrading. And yet I had just made use of it myself . . . by no means for the first time. Why the contradiction?

Without having to think too deeply about it, I knew the answer.

Shortly before her death, my wife Susan had spoken anxiously to me about the girls.

'If anything,' she had remarked suddenly, one evening when we were by ourselves, 'were to happen to me, you'd do your level best for them, wouldn't you?'

'Nothing's going to happen to you.'

'In that event, I'll still be around to boss the three of you. Nobody's immortal, though. For my own peace of mind, I'd just like to . . . Darling, I'm not suggesting you'd be consciously remiss in any way. But I do so much want them to have the opportunities I missed. I don't want them to grow up resenting their parents, like I did.'

'Heaven forbid. Can you see me denying either of them ballet lessons, if that was what they craved?'

Susan had given me a look that was not sceptical and yet at the same time fell a little short of wholly trusting. 'I don't want either Katie or Elaine ever to feel that they were . . . held back. That's so important to me. Can you understand?' she asked earnestly.

'I'm not entirely dense, love. Don't worry about it. Between us, we'll be giving both girls a leg-up whenever they need one.' I had grinned at her. 'You'll see to that.'

Two months later, Susan was gone. I was never sure whether she knew about the heart defect that carried her off, or whether its final onslaught was as cruelly unexpected to her as it was to us: what I did know was that it gave our brief exchange on the question of parental responsibility a poignancy and a significance that might otherwise have eluded me. At that time I was deputy editor of a tabloid evening paper based in the Midlands. The editor, who preferred a quiet life, left most of the production to me, and after a couple of years at the helm I had begun to form an affinity with the craft of potted news presentation: much against the prevailing tide, the *Heart of England Messenger* was performing well and improving steadily. I knew that I had a flair for the job, but after Susan's death I lost my way a little. I couldn't see which horizon I was making for, and I began drinking too much.

Elaine was twelve, and stagestruck. Katie, at fourteen, was scribbling verse and short stories and talking of a literary career. Both ambitions seemed of a hazardous nature, and I was in no position to lend unlimited support: school fees were costing me dear, and the slight problem of my drinking was a further drain upon my resources. For a year or more after losing Susan I was, on top of my grief, a severely agitated single parent. The girls, heading fast for adolescence, seemed likely to be needing material help for longer than at one time I had vaguely anticipated, and I couldn't see clearly where it was coming from. And, leaving aside my own inclinations in the matter, I had given in effect a solemn pledge: made a commitment. Thinking about it brought me out in a sweat, night after night.

One evening at the start of my second year as a widower, the annual awards dinner of the Press Owners' Association was held at a conference centre in Birmingham. Since the *Messenger* had been named as Brightest Provincial Tabloid and my part in its triumph could hardly have been overlooked, I found myself there as a guest. By some quirk of the seating arrangements, I was placed next to an individual of military bearing, aged around sixty, who was introduced to me as Sir Giles Horley, proprietor of the London *Announcer*, a City publication specializing in finance and the stock market, which had gained the accolade as that year's Most Improved Specialist Weekly. When he learned who I was, Sir Giles seemed anxious to talk.

During the meal, it emerged that although relatively new to the industry he had further newspaper ambitions. For a start, he was keen to spruce up the *Announcer*'s image still more. Had I, he demanded, any ideas?

Under the influence of the table wine, I offered a few suggestions. He seemed impressed. By the end of the main course, the cut and thrust of our discourse had reached a dizzying tempo, and at the conclusion of the evening he pumped my hand warmly, eyeing me with the intensity of a man sizing up the merits of a new mark of eight-cylinder saloon.

'If you should ever find yourself in London,' he boomed, as though mooting an occurrence so improbable as to be faintly comical, 'look me up, Mr Rodgers. We'll have another chat, humph? Enjoyed your company this evening. You've given me a few pointers.'

I said I was glad. 'Best of luck,' he added, with faint patronage, 'with that mouthpiece of yours . . . what is it, the *Messenger*? Does you credit, my boy. Keep up the good work. Don't lose your touch.'

I said I would try not to, thanked him, went home and forgot his existence.

Fifteen months later, out of the blue, I received a call. Sir Giles had just purchased the *Planet*, a tottering Fleet Street tabloid in dire need of an overhaul before it disintegrated. Was I prepared to drop everything, go to London and take over, with a free hand?

By then I was established as nominal, as well as de facto, editor of the *Messenger*; and so I hesitated. I was, in truth, a little suspicious. With the pick of Fleet Street to choose from, why had Sir Giles turned to me, a comparative unknown? Only later did I learn that the *Planet*'s new owner had kept a continuous stealthy eye upon my and the *Messenger*'s progress since our meeting, and had continued to be impressed. The terms he offered me were lavish. Within three days I had made my decision: within a month I had brought Elaine, then sixteen and more stage-crazy than ever, to the capital with me and launched my tilt at the newspaper world's most decrepit windmill. Katie, who was at university, remained in the Midlands.

Embarking upon the theatrical trail, Elaine tramped it for the next three years with zest but small reward, before catching a Fringe producer's eye and landing a worthwhile part or two, then sliding under the wing of Jimmy Maxwell, one of the theatre world's Coming Men. Throughout this time, I was able to support her as I could not have done had I remained in provincial exile. My pledge to Susan had been redeemed, at least partly.

Normally, the Fleet Street environment is no particular help to anyone with a drink problem. In my case, however, a new sense of achievement enabled me to scale things down.

The challenge of my task absorbed me, and on the domestic front I was less uptight.

Inside a year, the editorial policy I introduced and applied showed clear signs of having the desired effect. The *Planet*'s sales had doubled, and computer forecasts indicated a quickening of the trend. In Press circles, I was beginning to make my mark.

Occasionally, giving the okay to an especially seamy exposure or passing a front-page picture of more than ordinary provocation, I caught myself wondering what Susan would have made of it. Always she had taken a loyal interest in my work on the *Messenger*. But a streak of fastidiousness had run through her, and the reincarnation of the *Planet* under my direction might have proved a little harder for her to take. I wasn't sure. What I was certain of was that, with its aid, I was now in a position to fulfil her dearest wishes in respect of the girls: other things were secondary.

Which was not to say that I took no pride in the *Planet*'s performance. Four years after the re-launch, I had rationalized my attitude towards its function. Some called it a scandal-sheet. To me, it was a Crusader in gaily-painted armour.

A squawk from the intercom brought me back from the window.

'Someone to see you, Mr Rodgers,' announced Reception. 'A Mr Andrew Kent.'

'Bundle him up here, will you?'

The figure that presently arrived was above medium height, lean, fair-skinned, brown-haired, nudging early middle age. His handclasp was vigorous. Gesturing him into the visitor's chair, I said, 'You saw Wally Farr yesterday, I believe. He gave me a briefing on you.'

'I'm sure he did.' There was a dry directness to the reply. His voice hinted at Lancashire origins.

'The thing I'm not clear about—' I paused to scan him with the ghost of a grin that I held in reserve to soften loaded questions—'is why you want to leave the agency and join us. Doing quite nicely there, weren't you?'

Leaning back, he put the chair's armrests to use. 'The agency's been good to me,' he confirmed, weighing his words as if my query had forced him to go more deeply into his motives. 'I've made a lot of connections. But that kind of work . . . You know how it is. You get an assignment, you carry it out, the result gets sprayed around the media like fly-repellent and dissolves into a mist. Minimal job-satisfaction. Lately I've felt—'

'You'd appreciate,' I said, as he checked, 'an identifiable style of your own? A byline?'

'That puts it neatly. I do feel I've some aptitude for an investigative role—the sort that a tabloid can foster. I'd like,' he added, half-apologetically, 'to make a name for myself.'

'And feel you were doing something useful?'

His mouth widened as his face-muscles relaxed. 'That too.'

'What made you pick the *Planet*?'

He gestured. 'You're the high-flyer of this decade. The Phoenix. I'd like to be along for the ride. Also—' he sent me a quick glance—'I feel I've something of a personal stake in the *Planet*'s rise from the ashes.'

'How's that?'

'Through my daughter.'

'Ah. She works here?'

'No. But you gave her some prominence a few years back. You probably don't remember, but you ran a talent contest for youngsters as part of your early promotion campaign, and she—'

'I recall vividly. Sir Giles, my Governor, talked me into it. One of his better ideas. It was just after I took over here—our first shot in the circulation war. The contest winner . . .' I squinted. 'Jilly Kent, right? A fourteen-year-old sparkler . . . how could I forget? Very photogenic. We put her on the centrefold. Song and dance, a spot of mimicry—versatile, no question. Your daughter? Well, well. How's she doing now?'

'Carving her own career. But I don't think,' added Kent reminiscently, 'she ever forgot the start you gave her, and I—my wife and I—certainly didn't. So you see why I feel some involvement with the *Planet* and yourself.'

I bowed slightly from the waist. 'Always glad to be of service. But the real kudos, in this instance, has to go to the Governor. The contest was his brainchild.'

Kent gave a tolerant laugh. 'I dare say it did wonders for the sales figures. Which is what it's all about, let's face it.' He glanced again, perhaps to gauge my position. 'A canny gentleman, Sir Giles.'

'You're right,' I said neutrally.

'I bumped up against him recently, at the Newspaper Proprietors' lunch. He seemed to know exactly where he wants the *Planet* to go, and how to get it there.'

'Right again. Well, Mr Kent—'

'People call me Andy.'

'Don't worry. If you join us, you'll be called worse than that by the end of the first morning.' I hesitated. 'You're aware, of course, that we already have a chief crime man, Gil Purvis? If you did join the team, you'd be under him.'

Kent flapped a hand. 'Suits me. Gil and I have come into contact quite a bit. Incidentally, if it's a recommendation you're after . . .'

'That won't be necessary.' I didn't tell him that Wally Farr had been in touch with the agency and checked on his track record, to our entire satisfaction, twenty-four hours previously. 'As long as you're clear on the terms of reference, we can stitch things up right now. On the question of remuneration . . .'

Inside five minutes the details were settled. Kent went

away to make arrangements for starting with us in four days' time. After he had left, I buzzed Laura Cadey of the Woman's Page and asked her to see me when she had a moment.

CHAPTER 3

Despite doing his best to appear to be a hard-bitten news editor in the finest Fleet Street mould, Wally Farr was saddled with a personality that made him instantly likeable to everybody, to his chagrin. He carried a lot of surplus weight, and when he was amused, which was not seldom, much of it quivered. Most of the time, he took things just seriously enough to produce a newspaper.

Gil Purvis, who by contrast was scrawny and fast-moving, took things very seriously indeed. A discussion with the pair of them was therefore useful, providing a consensus. Having listened to them both in the course of an impromptu meeting at midday, I scratched my scalp and reflected.

'If there's anything in it,' I said finally, 'we'd best start revising our ideas. For safety's sake, maybe we should anyway.'

Purvis tapped his desktop with a ballpoint. 'Purely on the speculative side, I think it might be worth plunging. Granted, it's only what Edna Wallington told me, but I've no reason to doubt her word.'

'Any police comment?'

'Just the inevitable. Inquiries proceeding, all avenues being explored. What Edna says, though, is enough on its own to justify some kind of a spread, wouldn't you say?'

I sighed. 'I wasn't that anxious to keep hammering it. We've stuff by the mile crying out for space—right, Wally?' He wagged a solemn head. 'But if Sir John was in fact being threatened, or thought he was . . .'

'There's no real evidence,' Purvis said regretfully. 'According to the redoubtable Edna, her brother took both notes away with him and she never saw either of them again. But she insists that he looked shaken, each time.'

'She didn't actually read them?'

'No. But spotting his reaction, she asked about them. On neither occasion did she get a straight answer. He just muttered something about certain people taking a twisted view of things and not being worthy of attention. He didn't seem to want to discuss it.'

'Was that unusual?'

'It was his manner, she says, that was unusual. As if he'd had a knock to his self-confidence. Normally he was very sure of himself, totally committed to whatever project he was on. After getting these letters, he looked . . . insecure. She got the impression that for a while, in each case, he was looking at things unwillingly from a different slant. That's the best way she could describe it.'

I sniffed. 'But he never consulted the police?'

'They've no record of his having done so.'

With a glance at Wally, I said with some reluctance, 'It's just a shade too intriguing to disregard. We'll have to give it some prominence. Tell you what. Why don't we box it, bold-face, right across the front at the top, cut the rest to size and run it underneath? Wally? Any other ideas?'

'You know I don't have ideas. My function is to put constructive proposals into effect. Let's do that, and make everyone happy.'

'Except Dave Windsor,' remarked Purvis.

'There's no pleasing him at the moment.' I glanced at the newsroom clock. 'Okay, Gil. We'll leave it to you to work up as best you can. Voices from the past, the torment of men in the public gaze . . . all the hypothetical claptrap, right? Edna can't complain, she's surmising too. I've got to be off.'

At the doorway I paused. 'Did I mention, you'll have

Andy Kent joining you on Monday? I gather you're acquainted.'

Purvis nodded. 'Bright guy. Spent too long hiding his light under the agency bushel. He should prove useful.'

Laura Cadey was waiting in my office, seated on a corner of the desk and smiling at a revised proof which she had removed from my in-tray. A well-built brunette of about forty, she packed more sex-appeal than was even hinted at by the outdated photograph of her that sometimes stared out from her own page: I was always urging her to change it, but she said she wanted people to go on remembering her as thirty-five, with dimples. Dropping the proof daintily back into its receptacle, she transferred the smile to me. 'Sorry I couldn't get up here sooner.'

'That's okay. No panic.'

'We had a hysterical reader on the line. Yesterday's piece on slimming had really got to her. Apparently her daughter's anorexic, and she has this notion that people like us are bent on polishing her off. I'd have left her to Meg, only . . .'

'Only your kind heart wouldn't let you?' I patted her arm. 'These deluded types, they're all over the place, you can't avoid them. Now, why did I want a word with you? Oh yes. It's more relevant now than it was an hour ago. How fixed is your page-planning for the next few days?'

Laura's large, hazel eyes, a little dark-circled, regarded me with a certain wariness tempered by elements of trust. 'It's never that rigid, Peter, as I think you know. Why do you ask?'

'Might there be space to spare, tomorrow or Saturday, for a possible special feature? Subject: the surviving womenfolk of slaughtered celebrities.'

'*Apropos* Sir John Wallington?' she inquired instantly.

'He and one or two others. Those who've met recent sudden deaths. It occurred to me, an insight into how such traumas react upon their nearest and dearest . . .'

'I don't see why not,' Laura said slowly. 'Good idea. Meg could do it. She has the coaxing approach.'

'She'll need it. I think it could make something readable, don't you? John Wallington's sister is a must, for starters. Gil Purvis has already talked to her, so she's reachable.'

Laura made a note. 'And . . . ?'

'Mrs Paul Lewis. Widow of the scriptwriter. I believe we had a quote or two from her at the time. And it could be worth chasing up Linda Briggs.'

'Who's Linda Briggs?'

'She *was* the live-in girlfriend of Carl Scott, head of drama with Metropolis TV.'

'I'd forgotten about him. My word, what a holocaust in the arts world.'

I stared at her. 'You know, you've got something there. All three of them worked in entertainment. Odd thing.' I remained pensive for a moment, then headed for my chair. 'You'll get Meg on to it, then?'

'Right away.' Quitting the desk, she adopted a stance of consideration. 'She'll need all of tomorrow, I expect. Shall we aim for Saturday?'

'Fine. A weekend weepie. Got time for some lunch?'

'Now?'

'If you've a half-hour to spare. I want to tell you about Elaine.'

Laura's eyes radiated an understanding smile. 'See you in the canteen. Five minutes.'

Chipping at a slice of veal and ham pie, I said, 'You're right, of course. I do still miss Susan at times. How about another special feature on prematurely bereaved newspaper editors? At the rate we're going, we'll soon have to flog a box of Kleenex with every copy.'

Laura pulled a face. 'The girls are a consolation, though?'

'Can't think what I'd do without them. Elaine, of course,

in particular. She's still with me at home . . . so far.'

'And Katie? What's she up to? Penning her second novel?'

'At a hideout in the Cotswolds. She's rented this half-derelict cottage where she's been scribbling, supposedly alone, for the past five months. She keeps well in touch by phone.'

Buttering her roll, Laura took a meditative mouthful. 'That first book of hers was a humdinger. Think this one will match up?'

'If it doesn't, it won't be for want of raw material . . . and I do mean raw.'

'You've read it, then?'

'I've seen the synopsis and a couple of sample chapters. Well, Laura, you know me. Hardly the arch-prude of the printed syllable, would you say? But I did find myself wondering how I'd managed to rear a child with such fertile imagination.'

'As long as that's all it is.'

'Don't put ideas into my head. Ah me, the world moves on. One does try to keep up, though at times it's a struggle. I'm hoping Katie makes a fortune out of this one.'

'Why?'

'So I can sponge off her when newspapers are supplanted by instant linear feedback or whatever technology comes up.'

'You're better off as you are,' Laura said practically.

'Of course I am. Penthouse luxury with an adoring daughter whose only demand is that I watch her on stage about once in five weeks, using words I never taught her and displaying things I was only vaguely aware she had. Sons are less complicated, I imagine. See much of Gerald?'

She shook her head. 'He's still up at university; spends most of the vacations with his uncle. We write. Now and then he gives me a call, chortles over something I've published, informs me the real world isn't like that, then sinks back for another three months.' She gave me a wry look. 'We sound like a pair of hens, clucking over our departed chicks. Still, you do have Elaine . . . though for how long? What's he like, this brilliant young theatre director of hers?'

'Jimmy Maxwell? I've only met him once. Artistically he's rumoured to be one of the coming men. Physically he's a bit weird.'

'In what way?'

'He has this flowing raven hair that seems to have slid away from his forehead and regrouped behind his shoulder-blades. His eyes are slightly crossed and he has a stomach. He lurches a bit, as if one leg is shorter than the other.'

'He sounds like Quasimodo.'

'Well, he's certainly got Elaine in thrall. Hardly surprising, of course. He wields a certain amount of theatrical influence, and Elaine seems to have done nicely out of him so far. Only fringe productions, but you have to start somewhere.'

'Good luck to her,' declared Laura. 'I wouldn't mind seeing the new one.'

I gave her a stare. 'The two-parter at The Backstage? You're not serious?'

'Why shouldn't I be? I adore the theatre.'

'That's what I mean. If you're in earnest, though, be my guest for the evening. I'm always given free tickets, and I get tired of using the spare seat for my coat and umbrella. I once tried taking a neighbour of ours, but it wasn't a triumph. She's rather strait-laced. When Elaine made her entrance, took off most of her clothes and uttered the opening lines of what turned out to be the kind of dialogue they used to print on illicit presses in East End warehouses, for export, I knew we'd lost a friend. She doesn't call in for drinks any more. Not that I mind. I never cared for her much. Will you come?'

'Of course, I'd love to. I promise not to go taut.'

'You needn't write the notice. Ron Kershaw's seeing to that.'

'I'm sure he is,' Laura said artlessly.

Ten minutes after my return to the desk, the rounded tones of Wally Farr came through to announce an event. A body which had been found on a building site in Tottenham Court Road was reliably reported to be that of Melvyn Winters, current holder of the *Planet* Actor of the Year Award and star of the latest blockbusting sex/horror movie, *Night and Miss Peterson*. A chunk of concrete, precipitated from above, was thought to have been largely responsible for his injuries. Assuming the accuracy of both accounts, suggested Wally, yet another rethink of the front page seemed to be indicated, and would I care to come down and talk it over?

CHAPTER 4

After a forty-minute delay, confirmation arrived from Gil Purvis.

At one-thirty that morning, Mel Winters had been reported missing by his fiancée, actress and model Caroline Sharpe, when he failed to return to the Fulham house they shared. He had gone out at seven o'clock the previous evening to visit his elderly father at his Bloomsbury flat, saying he would be back by ten at the latest. At eleven, Caroline had telephoned the flat, to learn that Winters had left soon after nine, giving no hint of another appointment. After that she had contacted his agent and other associates, none of whom had seen him.

The discovery of the body was made at mid-morning by the operator of a mechanical digger on the site of an office block under construction on a corner site in Tottenham Court Road. While shifting a mound of rubble at the base of the foundation pit, thirty feet below street level, he had spotted what he took to be a heap of clothing . . . as in fact it was, with the addition of a human torso inside. The head had been crushed almost out of recognition. Identification was possible, however, by means of an abdominal scar and other marks vouched for by a distraught Caroline.

The body's position indicated that it had fallen or been thrown from the public observation platform provided by the contractors alongside the pavement overlooking the site. Unusually for such an amenity, the protective barrier was no more than chest-high and could conceivably have been scaled by a reasonably active person.

By the same token, somebody of average strength might have met with no great difficulty in heaving a man of Winters's slight build over the top of it. In view of the lack of evidence that the actor had harboured the faintest suicidal tendency, but on the contrary had every reason to be feeling on top of the world, the latter version seemed the less improbable.

'Besides which,' said Wally Farr, gazing across the shoulder of the front-page layout man who was dejectedly assessing the wreckage, 'the falling masonry seems to put the cap on it, so to speak. He could hardly have dropped it on himself.'

'Whoever did it, then, must have scaled the barrier, climbed down to the—'

'Not necessarily. Seems they'd also been digging up the footway nearby, left a few concrete slabs lying handy. All he had to do, our phantom killer, was lift a couple and hoist them over. Seeing they'd take the same line of descent as Winters himself, there was every chance of a direct hit.'

'Delightful.' The layout man gulped. 'How big a site picture do we want? If it's more than three-column width, that raises problems with the head-and-shoulders of Winters, which should go here on the left. By itself, we can get round that, but if we're trying to salvage something of the original plan . . .'

'We're not,' I decided. 'Agreed, Wally? This reinforces the Wallington story out of sight. We need the entire front for the pair of 'em. The rest will have to go inside.'

'No help for it,' Wally concurred.

Leaving the layout man to wrestle with the new concept, we headed back to Wally's cubicle. 'I'm assuming,' I said, 'Gil won't neglect to ask about possible threats delivered to Winters recently? If we could establish some link of that kind with Wallington . . .'

'Knowing Gil, he won't overlook it. But I'll see he gets a reminder, next time he checks in.'

'Aside from his dad, did Winters have any other family?'

'I believe not. This Caroline of his, she's shattered of course, but she's used to talking to the media so Gil may get some more out of her yet. We'll send someone to see the dad, too. It's just feasible that the reason Winters went to see him last night was to ask his advice about something that was bothering him.'

'On the other hand,' I demurred, 'if he'd been getting threats, would he have stopped after dark to study a building site, all by himself? Come to that, if there was an attacker, how did he do it without being seen? Tottenham Court Road is hardly the back of beyond.'

'The observation platform,' said Wally, 'is round the corner into the side-street. It's recessed into the hoarding, so it's hidden from the main road. Also, surprise surprise, the nearest street lamp had been vandalized.'

'*No Light on this Murder*,' I offered helpfully. 'That should fit nicely across six columns. No charge.'

Over a Scotch and a sandwich at Lacey's Bar, Gil Purvis filled in verbally the detail he had been obliged to omit from his story.

'It's Wallington all over again. Winters seems to have been a genuinely nice guy. No climb to success over the backs of others. The reverse. For a long time, he got left behind in the rush. When his break did finally come, everyone wished him well.'

'So they now affirm,' I said cynically.

Purvis shook his head. 'I believe what I've heard. He only landed the *Miss Peterson* role because it called for somebody self-effacing and relatively unknown . . . he fitted the bill in both respects. Prior to that, it's hard to see how he could have made enemies.'

'Who told you this? Caroline?'

'She and a dozen others. Not a dissenting voice. Up until that movie, he was a struggling third-stringer who was grateful for a stroll-on part in a TV washing powder commercial. Plus, he was known for helping out others even less lucky than himself.'

'Okay, he was a saint. Sudden success could have cracked his halo.'

'Nobody around him seems to have spotted the smallest difference, before and after.'

'Was he making another film?'

'Just finished one.' Purvis snapped his fingers. 'What's it called, now? *Hamish*. About a bisexual at large in Manchester. Very new-wave. Done with vast compassion and corresponding amounts of heavy breathing, from all reports. Reckoned to confirm his status as a giant talent, even if it doesn't do a bundle for conventional morality.'

'Neither did *Night and Miss Peterson*, as I recall. Disregarding its possible influence on the impressionable admass, it was a riveting piece of work—I don't wonder he rocketed to the top.' Draining my Scotch, I eyed Purvis speculatively. 'You're quite certain he hadn't received any threats on his life?'

'No, I'm not.' I gave him a second look, a harder one. He added, 'I haven't played anything down. Caroline was adamant there'd been nothing of the sort: said she'd have known if there had been. Ditto from everyone else.'

'Including his dad?'

'He's too broken up to talk, but from what the police managed to get out of him initially it seems his son's visit was purely social. No burdens unloaded. Sorry, Peter. That's how it is.'

'Then why aren't you convinced?'

Purvis rotated the remaining whisky in his glass, staring at it. 'Couldn't tell you,' he confessed. 'Maybe it was a look in Caroline's eye . . . something in her voice. I don't know. It left me with the shadow of an impression, that's all.'

'An impression of what?'

He shrugged. 'That she might have recalled something. Some incident too trivial to mention. I could be fantasizing. She didn't budge from her story, so I probably am. But I've had these feelings once or twice before.'

'And?'

Purvis smiled thinly. 'And I'm still crime dogsbody for the *Planet*, not head of Interpol, so there has to be something wrong with my chemistry. Just the same, there have been occasions when . . . how shall I put it? I've half made a note of things that later I've wished I'd put on tape.'

'Does this fall into that category?'

'Possibly.'

'So shouldn't you be out there, beavering away?'

Wearily he leaned back. 'If I could think of a further inquiry to make, I'd make it. Maybe you can suggest something?'

Laura had left the building, but Meg Saunders, her deputy, was still there. 'Just the girl I wanted,' I told her. 'How far have you got with the study of bereaved females?'

'I saw Edna Wallington this afternoon.' Meg's clear, detectably Scottish voice always reminded me, for some reason, of a psychiatrist's couch, although as it happened I had no personal experience of such an article of furniture. 'And I've an appointment to talk to Sharon Lewis this evening. Linda Briggs I'm having a spot of bother with.'

'Why, is she being obstructive?'

'She's not being anything. It's merely that I've not been able to reach her. I thought I'd leave her till tomorrow.'

'Can you fit in a fourth?'

'Who?' she asked cautiously.

'Mel Winters's girlfriend, Caroline Sharpe.'

There was a pause. 'Mightn't it be a bit soon?'

'If she refuses, we're no worse off. But I'd like you to have a try. Gil Purvis thinks she could be holding something back.'

'Like what?'

'Some hint to Winters, possibly, that he might be in danger. If so, you're the girl to ease it out of her. How far did you get with Wallington's sister?'

'She's a funny old stick. You have to hitch on to her waveband. Once I'd done that, we got along fairly well. You know, it's odd you should say that about Caroline Sharpe. Edna was telling me, these letters her brother received . . .'

'Did she come up with more detail?'

'I'm not sure how much you have already. I'm roughing out a piece now—you can have it in half an hour, okay?'

'Thanks, Meg. Good luck with Sharon this evening. You might ask her—'

'Whether her late husband received menacing mail through the post before he was killed? Count on me.' As my finger hovered on the cut-off switch, she added, 'Is this the main purpose of these interviews? Or do their personal stories interest you, as well?'

'Guilty, on both charges.' I flicked the switch.

For the next twenty minutes I wrestled with a proof of the Comment I had composed earlier. It had to do with media censorship, a topic which lately had been generating some heat on both sides of the House of Commons. Because it was an emotive issue, my typewriter had run away with me; the amendments that were needed amounted virtually to a re-write. By the time I had got rid of it, Meg's outline interview with Edna Wallington had reached me, and I turned my attention to that.

For a woman well into her seventies who had just lost her brother in unspeakable circumstances, her replies were crisply to the point.

QUESTION: Had your brother seemed jittery or absent-minded recently, as if there were something on his mind?
ANSWER: Briefly, a couple of times, after receiving the letters. Crank mail was nothing new to him, but these particular two did seem to disturb him more than usual.
QUESTION: Did he discuss them with you?
ANSWER: All he would say was that some people had a tendency to take things too much to heart. I asked to see the letters, but on both occasions he said I might find them upsetting and the best thing was to disregard them.
QUESTION: Could they have been embarrassing to him, in some way?
ANSWER: I doubt it. My brother had no secrets from me, I'm quite sure. But he was always protective of my feelings.

Meg had gone on to ask all the right follow-up questions, with results similar to those achieved by Gil Purvis. Momentarily disturbing though the letters may have been, on neither occasion had it taken long for Sir John to regain his customary good humour and devotion to his work, and apparently he had not felt it necessary to consult the police. Since his death, Edna had gone through some of his papers without coming across anything which, on the face of it, could have accounted for her brother's reaction. He might, she agreed, have destroyed the letters. She knew for a certainty that he had no enemies, inside his profession or out of it. On the contrary, he was the most popular and well-loved of men, concerned only with putting his talents to the best possible use in providing entertainment that also ranked as artistic accomplishment. No, she had never seen a film directed by her brother. She was not a devotee of the cinema, but she knew of the quality of his work by repute, and that was good enough for her.

Putting Meg's rough copy aside, I leaned back in my chair and gazed into vacancy for a while. Presently Wally Farr came through to request my presence in the newsroom, and with an untypical feeling of reluctance I answered the call. With editorial decisions waiting to be made, enigmas would have to keep.

CHAPTER 5

It was shortly past midnight when I reached home. An early night. Elaine, who had changed out of theatre garb and was encased in a kind of kimono of violent reds and yellows, over which her loosened hair cascaded like a peat-tinted torrent, met me in the hallway. 'Nearly a civilized hour, for once. Like a drink?'

'I'd prefer a night's sleep. But if you're having something . . .'

'We're on white wine. I'll fix you some.'

I gave her a bleary glance. '"We"?'

'Jimmy came in for a few minutes. He's always bringing me home,' she explained in a confidential whisper, 'so I thought it was high time he got something more than a good night at the door. Go in and say hallo.'

Reading my expression, she added quickly, 'If you'd sooner go straight to bed, Jimmy won't mind. I'll tell him—'

'Nonsense, darling.' Knowing his importance to her, I was prepared to make an effort, even after a fourteen-hour day which had been no less taxing than normal. 'I'll come through to be reintroduced. How did it go tonight?'

'Could have been worse,' she said disparagingly. 'Justin fell against the set and made a hole in it, and Babs forgot her lines twice, but we just about skirted disaster. Jimmy, you remember my father? Last time you met, most of the lights were out, everyone was half-tight and we were all trying to decipher the reviews in the first editions, so if you can't recall a thing about each other . . . Half a glassful, Dad? While I'm at it, I'll top us all up. Jimmy has to drive back, but one more shouldn't put him over the limit . . .'

Nervous about my reaction, she was talking uncharacteristically fast, laying down a verbal smokescreen. Pumping an excess of goodwill into my smile, I took Jimmy Maxwell's extended paw with a heartiness that induced a tilt of his oddly-shaped head, tipping the bulk of his unfettered black hair into an unpremeditated position about his small, triangular-lobed ears. My description of him to Laura had, I ascertained, been reasonably accurate, although I had neglected to mention the abnormal length of his arms which gave him a simian look. His age was anything between twenty-five and forty.

'Nice to renew acquaintance,' I told him, securing my release from his grip. 'Many thanks for ferrying Elaine. We appreciate it. I hear the play's a success.'

He thought about that. 'The play,' he pronounced finally, 'stinks.' He spoke, as I now recalled, in spurts, terminating each phrase with a scissors-like movement of the jaw. 'Critics were fooled. That was Elaine. She carries it.' He explored a pocket. 'Cigar?'

Whipping a slim pack from the inside of his buckled leather jacket, he proferred it as though trying to wheedle a famished pet into taking nourishment. Accepting a panatella, I let him ignite us both. 'The critics,' I said gravely, 'can sometimes be relied upon for help when you least expect it. I hope our man . . .'

'The dear old *Planet*,' said Elaine, returning across the room with a brimming glass, 'invariably turns up trumps where we're concerned. I wonder why?'

'If this is half a glass,' I said severely, taking a mouthful to be sociable, 'I'd hate to be with you when you're celebrating.'

'Drink it up. Do you good.' Perching herself on an arm of Maxwell's chair, into which he had lowered himself like cargo entering a hold, she placed a hand lightly upon the hair that had reassumed its rightful place across his nape. The director bore it with avuncular detachment. 'The thing is, Dad, will you be sending someone along to our first night at The Backstage? We're not asking, mind. It's up to you. Rick Smythe's a blazing talent, that's all, so we thought maybe—'

'Our drama section,' I assured her, 'has its finger on the pulse. I'm sure they won't overlook anything. What's your rating, Jimmy, of his latest? Chance of it moving to the West End later?'

Circular movements of the director's mouth suggested that he was pondering. 'Better than evens,' he came up with finally. 'Commercial and meaningful. Good mix.'

'Commercial,' Elaine translated helpfully, 'means that even by current standards it's an evening of utter filth. Sociologically, though, it does have the most incredible . . . Sorry, Dad. We're boring you rigid. How's the real world been today?'

'About par. Hear about Mel Winters?'

Her face contorted expressively. 'Isn't it *ghastly*? Poor Caroline. Apart from what she's feeling anyway, she's going to have to endure all kinds of nasty cracks. You know. Was Mel bent, and did he fall out with one of his boyfriends? It never fails. Poor kid, she's in for a rotten time. You've got your sleuths on the scent, I suppose?'

'Hardly the kind of story one can ignore,' I said gently. 'Especially so soon after John Wallington.'

Elaine displayed anxiety. 'What was I saying, only this morning? You laughed at me then.'

'Certainly not. I was just trying to keep a sense of proportion. If there's a pattern—which is hypothetical anyway—I don't regard people like myself as being part of it. I'm not in the movie business.'

'You're in the business of mass entertainment,' she murmured. 'Just as they were.'

'Hardly a fair comparison,' I protested. 'The prime function of the Press is to inform and educate.'

Elaine's disrespectful squeal echoed from the walls. 'The *Planet*? You're joking.'

'All right, so we dress it up a bit. But to draw a parallel between a news-sheet and a screen fantasy . . .'

'Well, never mind. It's all a matter of interpretation. The point is, no male notability of any kind seems to be safe in the streets just now . . . so watch it, Dad. You can't be too careful. Right, Jimmy?'

The dark eyes of the director, his most charismatic feature, were bulging slightly as if overloaded with the thoughts piling up behind them. He emitted a faint, unidentifiable noise. Evidently satisfied, Elaine gave his hair an ultimate vigorous rumpling before leaping up and hurrying to the antique bureau in a corner of the room.

'You see?' she demanded across a scarlet-and-yellow shoulder. 'Jimmy agrees with me, and he's had experience. Now where did I . . . ?'

Opening the bureau lid, she began to rummage. I said politely to our guest, 'You've been the victim of a street attack?'

His head shook. 'Brother of mine. Two years back.'

'I'm sorry. Was he badly hurt?'

'Only partly paralysed,' said Elaine tersely, from the bureau.

'That's awful. Can he get around at all?'

'He copes,' Maxwell said broodingly.

'Before the attack,' Elaine elaborated, returning with something in her hand, 'Jeff was a successful architect, wasn't he, Jimmy? Now, he can barely hold a pencil. He can't concentrate for more than ten minutes at a stretch. He lives in a sheltered unit and has practically everything done for him. You see what can happen to you? So take this,' she commanded, pressing a cylinder into my palm, 'and carry it around. Don't hesitate to use it. Promise?'

'Hairsprays are for woman,' I objected, studying it. 'If I'm found with this in my pocket, my reputation will fall apart. Besides, I'm not sure it's legal.'

'Quote me a law against possessing a can of Highlight Mist. It could save your life. Its muzzle-velocity is vicious, I can tell you, and if it gets in your eyes it'll blind you for an hour.'

'That's why it's prohibited.'

'So is murder,' Elaine said drily. 'If John Wallington had had one of those, he might not have left a grieving sister and a depleted film industry behind him. If Mel Winters had had one—'

'It would probably have confirmed everyone's suspicions. Would Jimmy carry one, if you asked him?' Notwithstanding his presence, it seemed natural somehow to refer to him in the third person. Elaine cast him a fond look.

'Jimmy takes his own precautions. Show Dad one of your party tricks, love.'

To my astonishment, Maxwell lifted himself compliantly out of his chair, turned, and picked it up one-handed. With a slight tightening of the mouth he raised it above his head, held it there for an instant, returned it effortlessly to carpet level and restored it to conventional usage. The chair, like the bureau an heirloom from Susan's side of the family, one of the things I had clung to when she faded out on us, was a massive affair of carved mahogany, requiring two hands and a foot just to slide it across the floor when either Elaine or I did the Hoovering. I looked hard at its occupant. His breathing seemed normal.

'I'm impressed,' I said feebly. 'Is there a knack to it?'

'Muscle-power.' Elaine's mouth betrayed an impish glee. 'Jimmy can smash walnuts between finger and thumb, no problem. It's inherited sinew. His grandad was a circus performer.'

Maxwell's freakish appearance and addiction to theatre were starting to be accounted for. Coming swiftly to terms with the revised scenario, I addressed him directly. 'With that background, I'd have thought you'd be happier as a performer yourself.'

He smiled faintly. Elaine said with a degree of tact, 'He feels he lacks personality. Can't project.'

Leaving aside his somewhat outlandish aspect, the real reason, I suspected, was that Maxwell liked to be in control of others. Dumping my wineglass, I turned back to them with what I hoped was an air of benevolence. 'Well, henceforth I shall have no qualms about Elaine when she's with you. Glad to meet you again, Mr Maxwell. Okay—Jimmy. Call round any time. Now you'll have to excuse me, I'm starting to blur at the edges. I'll leave you to talk drama. 'Night, darling.'

On tiptoe for a kiss, Elaine whispered, 'How about that spray?'

'It was a nice, filial thought, and I love you for it.'

'Yes, but will you carry the thing?'

'If I can find room for it,' I temporized.

She sighed. 'I think I'm wasting my time. And my Highlight Mist. Anyhow, take *care*. Oh—a message from Katie. She phoned at lunch-time. Tell Dad, she said, to watch out for muggers: they seem to be turning their sights on well-heeled gentry in the public gaze. So it's not just me, you see, imagining things.'

I flipped a comic glance Maxwell's way. 'Don't ever have two daughters,' I advised him, 'unless you feel you can handle a brace of leading ladies at the same time. They're apt to take over.'

Generally speaking, vocational pillow-thought was not something that plagued me. On the rare occasions when sleep remained out of reach, I normally avoided adding to the discomfort by reflecting upon all the items I might have published and hadn't, or those I had and shouldn't have. The process was self-defeating, one to be shunned.

Thoughts did, of course, flutter around. Sometimes they were about Susan. By now I could give them house-room, because I was over the hump. Eight years are almost a hundred months, which is a lot of weeks in which to grind pain to a powder, sharp-grained but inert. Remembering Susan as she had been before the final month or so was something akin to a moral obligation: if one didn't recall the good times, what was the point of their having existed?

On this particular night, it wasn't Susan. Notwithstanding my flippant response to Elaine's forebodings, I wasn't a Pressman for nothing: I could spot the emergence of a pattern when it showed itself. Already, with the aid of my team, I was doing my best to exploit it. As far as that went, I wasn't disposed to fault Elaine's reasoning.

Where her view and mine diverged was at the point marking my own status as a possible victim. Newspaper editors, as I had tried explaining to her, could hardly be said to fall into the same category as screen idols. In my own case, a slight deviation from this general rule could perhaps be discerned, in that a fair amount of media publicity had been given in recent years to the switchback fortunes of the *Planet* and my success in injecting it with the will to live. While claiming no special magic, I did have faith in my assessment of what a sizeable slice of the reading public looked for in a national tabloid daily. Granted my free hand by the Governor and an amenable Board, I had got results. As far as my immediate professional circle was concerned, I was regularly the flavour of the month, and doubtless would remain so for as long as the injections continued to do the trick.

Nothing of this, however, could have made me a household name, let alone a face. To the ordinary man, a daily newspaper is a bunch of printed sheets that appears every morning in his letter-flap; those behind its arrival remain phantoms. Had I been called in to resurrect an ailing TV channel, my features and hairstyle would have been public property, my smallest mannerisms known to every schoolchild. As string-plucker on the fifth floor of Planet House, I could have worn green lipstick and brass bells on my shoulders, for all that anyone outside my immediate ambit would have known or cared.

For this reason, I didn't subscribe to Elaine's apprehension on my behalf. So why, on this particular night, was I lying sleepless, irked by mental rumblings that refused to surface for identification?

At three a.m. I switched on the bedside lamp.

Propping myself up, I smoked the remaining portion of Jimmy Maxwell's cigar and strove to come to grips with whatever was lurking.

Subconscious guilt?

Was something trying to tell me that I shouldn't be inciting my staff to hound victims' relatives for story purposes? It was a trifle late in the day for such scruples. Nothing of the kind had troubled me before. The view I took was that, in the event of the mark being overstepped, the kickbacks would speedily make themselves felt: unless and until this happened, everything and everybody was fair game. If I hadn't felt this way, what remained of the *Planet* would long since have taken its final step to destruction.

Uneasiness, then, over something I should have spotted and hadn't? Some story-angle that had eluded me?

I didn't think so. Any deficiency of this kind on my part would in any case have been made up by Wally Farr or one of the others. From the start, I had taken care to surround myself with people who were adroit at detecting possibilities. We worked as a team. Our coverage of the killings so far, I felt convinced, had lacked nothing of significance.

My thoughts strayed towards Mel Winters and his gruesome end. In the buzz of a newsroom, such incidents are neutered into mere column-fodder, the overtones drowned. Supine on a mattress at three in the morning, I found myself picturing the event and yielding to a shudder. Although I knew nothing of Winters except what I had read and seen, the conviction took hold of me suddenly that everything people had been saying about him was in all probability true: he was a nice little guy upon whom fortune had briefly smiled, there was no reason for him to have been killed, and yet despatched he had been, with cruelty and senselessness, and something about the occurrence failed to add up. It was John Wallington over again, an action replay, with an added dimension of the macabre. I saw the slight figure of the actor being seized from behind, bundled over the barrier, plunging thirty feet into the pit, lying there stunned while, coolly and methodically, the killer collected a pair of eighteen-inch concrete slabs and dropped them on his head. What kind of an exit was that?

Crushing the cigar, I switched off the lamp and turned on to my side, trying to wrench my mind clear of the one-way track. But it was another hour before I drifted into sleep, and then I dreamt I was being chased. It didn't help that I couldn't see the pursuer's face; nor that Elaine, or somebody female, was in the vicinity, shrieking at me.

CHAPTER 6

'I think,' said Laura, 'she's made quite a decent job of it. See how it strikes you.'

Meg Saunders could write. She had a gift for the arresting phrase. She was, besides, a first-rate interviewer with an aptitude for rooting out detail that might have escaped others. It was therefore with some optimism that I scanned the proof of her completed feature, provisionally headlined *The Women They Left Behind*. I was left with a sense of disappointment.

Observing my reaction, Laura said loyally, 'With a little more time, Meg could have managed something in depth. Four interviews of that kind in a day and a half . . .'

'It's fine,' I said promptly. 'I've no criticism.'

'Only it's not quite what you were looking for?'

'If you could tell me what I'm looking for, I'd be more than grateful. As a topical feature on feminine bereavement, this could hardly be bettered. I guess I was hoping for the impossible.'

'More of a pointer,' Laura suggested shrewdly, 'from Caroline Sharpe, perhaps?'

'Could be. Gil Purvis had this feeling about her, and I have this pathetic faith in Gil's journalistic antennæ. Still, there it is. I'm sure Meg did all she could.'

'She'll be back from tea in twenty minutes. Why not ask her yourself?'

Presenting herself in my office a quarter of an hour later, Meg affirmed that everything she had wormed out of Caroline Sharpe was there in her copy. 'If she was protecting her boyfriend's name—trying to cover up some character defect or skeleton in the cupboard—then she's missed out on her vocation, that's all I can say. For my money, she was being utterly frank. Mel Winters really was a well-loved member of the acting fraternity with nothing to hide. We can all keep our illusions about him.'

'So you think it *might* be an illusion?'

'I didn't say that,' she said reprovingly. 'I'm talking generally. Most people nurse impressions of some kind, don't they, about screen idols? Part of the mythology.'

'This house in Chelsea . . . How long had he been living there with Caroline?'

'Getting on for a year.'

'Were they planning to marry?'

'In the sense that they weren't contemplating a split, I suppose you could say they still had matrimony vaguely in mind.'

'Will Caroline go on living there?'

Meg gave me a guarded look. 'Is that something I should have asked?'

'Not necessarily. Thanks, Meg, for a top-class effort. Take the weekend off.'

'I was going to, as it happens.'

With a slim Saturday edition on the brink of production and the prospect of a day's respite to follow, Wally Farr was starting to wear his end-of-the-week mantle of total relaxation. At my inquiry, a change threatened his manner.

'You're not about to put up some fresh hare?' he queried suspiciously. 'We've just got the front nicely settled.'

'Take it easy, Wally. I only wondered if Gil might be available for something not especially urgent I have in mind.'

'Barring emergencies, he's tied up for the next week. The Town Halls probe,' he reminded me, seeing my vacant expression. 'It's boiling up. There's some sex in it, you'll be relieved to hear. A couple of dishy secretaries have spilled the beans, and there's more to come. Gil's hot on the trail.'

'Good. Pictures?'

For answer, Wally pushed across a selection of full-plate prints. Having riffled through them, I gave an applauding nod. 'Obviously we can't let up on that, now. Much too spicy. Okay, we'll leave Gil out of this.' I snapped my fingers. 'I've just remembered. This new man's joining us on Monday—Andy Kent, late of the agency.'

'So he is. You want to lay claim to him?'

'If you've no objection.'

'Take him,' Wally said expansively. 'I'd forgotten he was coming, to be honest.' Curiosity got the better of him. 'Tell me something, Peter. Is there an aspect of the Winters/Wallington story that's escaped my attention? I only ask because it's rare for you to—'

'Relax. You're not losing the razor edge of your news-sense, so far as I know. I'm indulging myself, that's all. It'll come to nothing.'

Saturday was normally a quiet day for me. This time around, I had been hoping for a few uninterrupted hours in the company of Elaine. However, she had a morning rehearsal, and I knew she would want to spend the afternoon shopping before making her way to The Peacock for the evening's two performances. Top-floor Fringe or not, Elaine took her stage commitments seriously and I respected her attitude.

Reconciled to solitude, I made a virtue of necessity and followed up a leisurely late breakfast by installing myself at full length on the studio couch, partly shielded from the shrill glare of an April morning sun, and dipping unhurriedly into the range of offerings supplied by the opposition. This luxury came my way just once a week. For the rest of the time, it was a case of snatched glances in odd moments, purely in an attempt to stay in touch.

The Town Halls corruption story, I was gratified to find, had remained a *Planet* exclusive. This, combined with the provocative Diaries of Lady M, meant that we had cleaned up rather more comprehensively than usual; despite a native streak of caution, I couldn't help anticipating with a certain complacency the latest circulation figure, due on Monday. The *Record*, I noted with amusement, was publicizing some forthcoming Diaries of its own. They were reputed to have been obtained, at vast cost, from a head chef, and to contain 'revelations' (undefined) concerning the clientele of a certain fashionable restaurant in South Kensington. The *Record*, our closest rival, usually contrived to do better than this. Bob Dawson, its newly-promoted whizzkid editor, was manifestly panicking a little. Feeling soothed, I turned the page.

Immediately I stiffened. The main page three story, streamed across all six columns, was about Mel Winters, and although this was not unexpected I was less prepared for its content.

The gist of it was that Winters might have been distressed about something. The assertion was based upon an interview which the *Record*'s chief crime reporter had obtained with the actor's agent, a dynamic young man called Appleton. Although Gil Purvis had not overlooked such an obvious line of inquiry, either he had failed to elicit this statement of opinion or the *Record*'s crime man was making it up. Alternatively, and more probably, the latter had asked a lucky question and then flogged the answer for considerably more than it was worth. Morosely I read on.

'There's no doubt,' Mr Appleton told me, 'Mel wasn't quite himself. On the surface he was as cheerful as ever. But I could sense that something had happened to disturb him.'

Regarding the star's personal life? Mr Appleton denied this. 'Mel and Caroline had a good relationship, I'm certain. It's more likely to have concerned his career. But he didn't confide in me.'

However, added Mr Appleton, on one recent occasion Winters had asked him 'earnestly' whether he felt that a scene in his new film could be justified in artistic terms or whether it had been inserted for commercial reasons. 'I told him that if he didn't like the script he was in a strong enough position to make a protest, but that he should think carefully about it first.'

And did he? 'I assume so. The matter wasn't mentioned again, and he went on making the film.'

But he still seemed unsettled? 'Well, I think I knew him pretty well, and I'd say something was nibbling at him.'

There was more, in similar vein. Overall it didn't amount to much, except that it had given the headline-writer the chance to demand: DID SCREEN STAR DIE FOR A PRINCIPLE? The logic of the deduction was confused, since it seemed to point more in the direction of suicide than that of the murder which indubitably had occurred; but it did add up to an intriguing item, and it was irritating to find my own vaguely-formulated thoughts on the matter echoed so outspokenly by the enemy. I was reading the story again, swearing softly, when Elaine came bustling in and suggested coffee. I looked up in surprise.

'Great idea. I didn't expect you back this early.'

'The rehearsal was scrapped.' She struck a pose in the centre of the room. 'Ta-ra! We're all so perfect, Jimmy decided it wasn't necessary. Actually there was a mix-up in the bookings and we couldn't have the room, but the outcome is the same. Six hours of glorious freedom.'

'Congratulations. Get brewing.'

On her return with the tray I said, 'I didn't rate Jimmy as the type to be deterred by a mere lack of rehearsal space.'

Elaine poured the coffee, her hair collapsing in coppery confusion about her cheeks as she stooped to take aim. 'Just now, all he can think about is Rick Smythe and The Backstage. He's glad of any excuse to trot over there and do a recce.'

'Doesn't he want you along?'

'That'll come later.' Handing me a cup, she thrust hair out of her sightline and gave one of her sniffs. 'Hard work ahead . . . just by way of a change.' Before straightening up, she paused to inspect the newsprint on my lap. 'Still flogging Mel, I see. Tough on Caroline. She'll be taking it hard, if I know her.'

I glanced up. 'I wasn't aware you did?'

'Caroline? We were together at drama school. We once auditioned for the same TV commercial, don't you remember? She was the lucky one. No, it wasn't luck. They were after a brunette.' Sitting down with her cup, Elaine gazed reminiscently into space. 'She had to open a door with a tube of Blitz in her right hand and a wand in her left hand and say, It's Magic!—and then she was swallowed up in a whirlwind that swept away the fingermarks on the paintwork. Screen time: one-point-eight seconds. She earned enough from that to have five days in Lanzarote.' Burying her face in the cup, Elaine kept it there for several moments before emerging with an appreciative gasp. 'Needed that. Lack of breakfast catching up with me. How's the opposition today?'

'Treading on our heels.' Taking a ginger biscuit, I crunched pensively through half of it, giving her a sidelong survey. 'So you and Caroline are acquainted. Are you still in touch?'

'Christmas and birthdays, on and off.' Elaine peered at me darkly. 'What's in your mind?'

'I was wondering—'

'No.'

'Give me a chance—'

'I'm not doing a sneaky interview with her on behalf of the nosiest rag in Fleet Street. That's not what friends are for.'

'Did I suggest it?' I asked placatingly. 'We've already

spoken to her—twice. What did occur to me was, you might be considering getting in contact with her to offer your—'

'Done it already. I phoned yesterday evening and we had a little long-range sob. She wanted me to go round, for company, but I couldn't. I had to show up at The Peacock. She understood that.'

I put my cup down carefully. 'You're free until this evening.'

'You mean, I'd have loads of time to see her this afternoon?' Elaine wagged a finger at me. 'The same applies, you know. I may have a barnstorming editor for a father, God help me, but nothing would induce me—'

'I'm not asking that. It's something else . . . something perfectly harmless, believe me. Reasonably so, that is,' I appended, catching the glint in her eye. 'Mind if I just mention it to you?'

CHAPTER 7

By Monday, attention had begun to switch.

In the absence of further disclosures, the Winters/Wallington story had cooled to a solidity that would have needed white heat to restore it to fluid form, and barely a candle was available. Inquests on both men had been opened and adjourned. The prime cause of death in each case was given as head injuries, which hardly ranked as a surprise. Police requests for indefinite time in which to pursue inquiries had been granted. Rival sensations were jostling for position.

Chief among them, as far as Wally Farr was concerned, was the Town Halls scandal, now spreading its net to include narcotics in addition to sex. Happy as a lark, Wally was content to leave other things to me. Over a welcoming drink at lunch-time, I explained the situation a trifle apologetically to our new man, Andy Kent from the agency.

'Gil Purvis has it all at his fingertips. He likes tackling this sort of thing in his own way, so we tend to give him his head. Which leaves you free, for the moment . . . so I'm taking the liberty of claiming your services for what you might call a personal crusade. It won't always be like this, let me assure you.'

Kent said agreeably, 'I've not joined the *Planet* to behave like a prima donna. I expect to be assigned.'

'But you might also expect to be sent after hard facts.'

'Not always. Let's have it.'

With some diffidence, I said, 'I dislike the word *hunch*, but it's the only way to describe what I'm chasing. And I say "personal" because I have to plead guilty to using family resources in furtherance of a *Planet* investigation.'

Kent nodded intelligently. 'You'd like to know,' I went on, 'just what the heck I'm drivelling about? It's this. I happen to believe there's more behind the killings of Sir John Wallington and Mel Winters than meets the eye. In my view, there's a link. You saw the *Record* piece, Saturday?'

'Yes. They seem to think—'

'Those quotes from Winters's agent set my mind alight. What he said, you see, tallies so uncannily with what Gil Purvis dug up last week about Wallington. We were planning to lead on it. Then Winters copped it and we had to re-cast the page, so the Wallington aspect rather dropped out of sight. Now, the *Record* seem to have revived the issue.'

Kent raised an eyebrow. 'Wallington had seemed disturbed, as well?'

'To an extent.' I related what his sister had told us. 'You could put it down to fancifulness, of course, on Edna's part. Her brother might simply have been preoccupied once or twice with the movie he was making—having production problems or whatever. On the other hand, if it was that, why be secretive about it?'

'So as not to worry her?' Kent speculated.

'According to her, she'd always shared his difficulties in that respect. No, this was something a little bit out of the ordinary. Not soul-shattering, perhaps, but enough to cause hiccups in his tranquillity. Much the same as in Winter's case, if what his agent says is true. Strikes me as quite a coincidence. Which is why I roped in my daughter, Elaine.'

This time, both his eyebrows shot up. 'How was she able to help?'

'As luck would have it, she knows Caroline Sharpe. I sent—I encouraged her to call round on Saturday afternoon, bearing sympathy. I didn't want any harassment,' I said piously, 'so all I asked Elaine to do was to keep on the alert while she was in the house, put a few tactful questions if she thought fit, but mainly do her level best to steal a look at any of Winters's personal effects that might be accessible. In the event, she was lucky.'

'Caroline had found something?'

'No. But for the sake of something to do, she had been sorting through his things and was quite glad of a spot of help to clear the decks. Winters seems to have been something of a squirrel. There was a mass of stuff, including correspondence dating back twenty years, so you can imagine the chaos. Elaine spent a couple of hours helping to collate it.'

Kent looked baffled. 'But if nothing significant was found . . .'

'By Caroline, it wasn't. She was too upset to take much heed of anything. Elaine, though, noticed this.'

Having studied the envelope I passed him, Kent extracted with caution the sheet of notepaper it contained. After reading for a moment, he glanced up.

'Thought-provoking,' he agreed. 'I wouldn't go further than that.'

'Neither would any reasonable person. In the circumstances, it's an item of some interest, that's all. To a person like me, that is. Whether the police would be impressed is another matter.'

Kent sucked in his cheeks. 'In the circumstances, they might.'

Taking the letter back, I shook my head. 'Doubt it. The tone of the thing is a bit stronger than usual, it's true, and a sensitive soul might well be jolted by it, but it doesn't contain threats, specifically. Everything's implied. That's what I find fascinating about it. If you study the wording carefully, it's very cleverly put together, in a way that's calculated to cause maximum mental restiveness within certain limits. Reading it is like . . . like being nudged in the ribs with a stick of explosive. No real harm intended, probably—but can you be certain?'

'I see what you're getting at. Yes, you're right: it *is* clever.' Kent met my eye. 'What do you intend doing with it?'

'For the time being,' I said blandly, 'I'm inclined to treat it as something relatively innocuous that came into our hands by chance, providing the basis of a few desultory inquiries. If in due course it seems to acquire greater relevance . . .' I coughed. 'We'd naturally do our public-spirited duty and hand it over to the authorities.'

'These desultory inquiries,' Kent said, poker-faced. 'Is this where I come in?'

'How could you possibly have guessed? I want you, Andy, if you will, to spread the net a little.'

'In which direction?'

'Two ways, for a start. You remember Paul Lewis, the scriptwriter?'

'I covered the murder case in January.' Kent looked up sharply. 'You're not saying . . . ?'

'Lewis wrote scripts for several of the top TV serials, notably *Mayhem* and *The Tormentors*. As you know, they placed him firmly in the sex-and-violence bracket, and in-cidentally made his name. Then there was Carl Scott . . .'

'The guy responsible for all those New Wave productions on Channel Eight?'

'The ones they asked questions about in Parliament. Rotting the moral fibre of the country, and all that. He met his comeuppance while he was actually working on a new series at his home in Kilburn. Were you on that, too?'

'No, but it sticks in my mind. Early Feb, wasn't it?' Kent's glance became quizzical. 'It's April now. What happened in March?'

'The killer took a month off. It's wildest speculation,' I acknowledged, signalling to the barman. 'The fact remains, all four of the people we're talking about were prominent in the entertainment industry, and in the space of a few months all four have been wiped out for no tangible reason. Granted, the killing method has varied. Just the same, I don't see how anyone can deny that a thread exists.'

Kent looked thoughtful. 'I take your point. All right, thanks, another half of bitter. So, in the cases of Lewis and Scott, you want me to root out whatever I can in the way of, um, vaguely hostile notes which they may or may not have received a short while before their deaths? Wouldn't that have been done at the time?'

'Did it occur to you, in connection with Lewis?'

'No, but the police—'

'As I recall, both cases were officially treated as murder for profit. Silverware was taken from Scott's study. Lewis's wallet was missing.'

'Wallington wasn't robbed.'

'Granted. Neither was Winters. As I said, the cases differ . . . but the link remains.' I leaned back. 'You look dubious. Think the scent might be too cold to pick up?'

Kent took a gulp of his replacement half-pint. 'Lewis,' he said pensively, 'had a mother who worshipped him. If she's still around, I could have another crack at her.'

'Good. And Scott?'

'His girlfriend at the time . . .'

'Our Meg Saunders saw her on Friday. Tight-lipped. Anyone else occur to you?'

Kent pondered. 'Didn't he have a brother?' he said at last. 'I believe he was interviewed by a colleague of mine from the agency. He might be worth approaching again.'

'D'you mind?'

'As the new boy around here,' he reminded me, 'I'm not yet in the business of picking and choosing.'

'I'd feel happier if you were *keen* to do it.'

He laughed, genuinely amused. 'My sole aim is to bring joy into the life of my editor.' He buttoned his jacket. 'If I'm to get results, I'd best make a start. I'll check in with progress reports.'

During the afternoon I had a call from Katie.

'I'm in Town,' she announced. 'Came up to see Anna, and decided to make a few days of it. Can you cram dinner into your schedule this evening?'

'I do eat, my dear, quite frequently. Love to see you. Are you staying with us at the apartment?'

'I've made my own arrangements.' Katie sounded evasive: I guessed that someone in addition to Anna Beatty, her literary agent, was involved. 'Didn't want to shake up your routine. I'm ringing from the apartment, actually, but I'll be off shortly. Elaine and I have been having a Serious Chat. I hear you're refusing to carry your non-nuclear deterrent.'

'Your small sister fusses a little, don't you think? It's the theatre in her.'

A snort travelled down the line. 'Elaine may dramatize at times, but in this instance I agree with her. Better to overdo the precautions than finish up as an obituary on your own leader-page. Things don't always happen to other people. Who said that?'

'You did, this very minute.'

'I was quoting you. Editorial Comment, *Safety in our Streets*, five weeks ago.'

'That was a general argument, calling attention—'

'It was a perfectly valid cautionary tale, applying to you as much as to anybody else. Seriously, Dad. You can't dispute that things have been happening in London, just lately. As an eminent journalist you could easily be in the front line, so watch it. Lug that hairspray with you. One blast at the optic nerve, it's lethal. Now then—dinner. The Gourmet Platter, seven-thirty?'

We settled on that. Since the owner of Chelsea's currently most prestigious eating-house could claim a distant relationship to the *Planet*'s proprietor, Sir Giles, a bond existed between his establishment and ours, and a loose arrangement had evolved whereby it was understood that, in emergencies, messages could be transmitted and received without hassle. In return, we had spread the word to the rest of Fleet Street, elements of which gave the Gourmet their custom from time to time. The notion of meeting Katie there was a pleasurable one, and I still had a silly smile on my face when a tap on the door preceded the arrival of Laura, smartly decked out in a checked suit that did its utmost for her sturdy figure, and clasping a sheaf of galley-proofs. From the open doorway, she lobbed me a questioning glance.

'Just thought up a joke for the Comment tailpiece?'

'One doesn't jest on consecrated ground.' I beckoned her inside. 'Problems?'

'I need your OK on this.' Detaching the topmost proof, she flattened it over my blotter. While I scanned it, she sat in the interview chair and gazed over my head at the water-colours pinned to the wall behind me. When I looked up, she said, 'Some of those are Katie's, aren't they?'

'The harbour views.' I swivelled my own chair to eye them. 'She had an artistic bent before developing a literary bent . . . or a taste for bent literature, if you prefer.'

'They're good,' Laura adjudicated. 'If books ever fade out on her, she'll have a fall-back.'

'Seems unlikely they will. I've just been talking to her on the blower. She sounds buoyant. Here to see her agent, so I fancy the new opus must be about ready for launch. God help us.'

'Exciting time for her,' remarked Laura, tactfully skirting the topic of the book itself. 'What with her, and now Elaine poised on the brink of stardom, you've a pair of high-fliers in the family and no mistake. Now, about that piece of Meg's. Would you say it's pushing things rather?'

I shook my head slowly. 'I like the idea. A glimpse of the effect of an ambitious man's lifestyle on his long-suffering family—can't be dull, can it? Great appeal to the average woman. I do just wonder . . .'

'Whether now's the time?' she prompted.

'Well . . . In view of recent events, something like this might not rank as the height of diplomacy.'

'Quite honestly, Peter, I doubt if there's anything there that would trample on anyone's feelings, to that extent. And really they can't complain. All four of them said what's attributed to them. Meg's invented nothing.'

'She'll never reach the top,' I said drily. I took another look at the proof. 'Suppose we sit on this, say, for a week? It won't date. For the moment, I'd like to give Andy Kent a clear run with some inquiries he's making for me. He may have to approach one or two of these people again. If so—'

'I'll tell Meg,' said Laura, rising decisively. 'Didn't waste any time, did you, getting Andy on the job? How's he making out?'

'Very keen. Gets results.'

'I could have told you he would.'

'Not that the results add up to much, so far. What makes you such a talent-scout?' I asked teasingly.

'Merely the fact,' she replied with dignity, 'that I can

claim a closer acquaintance with Andy than a few others I could name. Actually it was his wife I knew first. Janet and I were on *Feminine Front* together for quite a while.'

'I didn't know that. Is she still there?'

Laura looked at me sadly. 'She's dead, poor girl.'

'Oh Christ. I'd no idea. When did she . . . ?'

'Three years ago. He doesn't like to talk about it. She was killed in a car accident—swerved into a tree. Nobody else involved. She was by herself at the time. Andy was shattered. That's partly why he likes to keep busy, though he's the conscientious type anyhow.'

'So I'd noticed. Well, thanks for putting me in the picture, Laura. I'll have to avoid foot-in-mouth remarks.' For a moment or so I stared bleakly ahead, remembering a few that well-meaning or regardless souls had blurted out to me. When my attention returned to Laura she was regarding me with a faint smile that implied understanding and a certain amount of fairly brisk compassion.

'I'll acquaint Meg, then,' she repeated, 'with what we've decided.' Without another word she left the office.

After a five-minute interlude for reflection, I applied myself to the following day's Comment before descending to the newsroom to ascertain how the Town Halls were shaping up. Wally Farr was looking content.

'Three chief executives,' he reported smugly, indicating a page-proof. 'Plus, a Mayor's female secretary, nubile and lens-rewarding. A revelation a minute, and more to come. I think we made the right decision.'

'You made it,' I reminded him. I skim-read the front-page text. Incontestably it was enjoyable stuff. 'How many pages have you allocated?'

'Four, provisionally. The pictures—'

'Yes, I agree, they're too good to skimp on. Have we left space for the Wendy Murray confessions?'

Ten minutes of debate cleared the way to a rough schedule

of priorities that, barring the unforeseen, would dominate our activities for the next few days. I had found this a good system. Adaptability to events was vital, but a basic programme formed the bedrock of the *Planet*'s new-found prosperity and maintained the purr in the collective throat of the Board.

Loudest of all, these days, sang the Governor himself. Sir Giles had never been one to play down his own achievements. And I had been, after all, his personal discovery. He alone had lifted me out of obscurity to take over: such success as I attained reflected upon him. While things went well, any methods I chose to adopt were likely to pass muster. Unhappily, it was not unknown for him to lob in the occasional lunatic proposal of his own. Astute as he may have been on the business side, his news sense could only have been described as eccentric. Skating around such periodical hazards was a manœuvre I was starting to master, albeit it took time and effort that I could ill afford.

Talking to Wally, I remembered with sudden dejection that the following evening was marked down as one of these dread occasions. Sir Giles had invited me to dinner at his Surrey retreat. Almost certainly this meant that he had hatched another idea. I didn't look forward to fending it off.

In the meantime, however, there was Katie.

'I'm away soon,' I told Wally. 'If need be, you can get me at the Gourmet. I'll be feeding my elder daughter.'

'Some people get all the breaks.'

'There are troughs, don't forget, as well as peaks. Tomorrow I'm guest of the Governor.'

Wally bent a compassionate eye upon me. 'Try not to think of your buddies here, wolfing ham rolls over the galley proofs.'

Driving through traffic whirlpools to the Gourmet, I thrust Sir Giles to the back of my mind and concentrated on enjoyable anticipation of my evening with Katie. I hadn't seen her in four months. This evening, at least, was going to be one for the scrapbook.

CHAPTER 8

'I'm a little bothered,' said Katie, 'about Elaine.'

Jolted, I dropped egg-yolk from my fork. 'In what way?'

Inserting a ball of wine-drenched melon between her teeth, Katie chewed dreamily for a few moments before getting rid of it. 'Hasn't it struck you?'

'If I knew what you were referring to . . .'

'This obsession of hers with that freak—what's he called?'

'Jimmy Maxwell?' I relaxed. 'He's a misshapen oddity, I grant you, but I wouldn't get too steamed up about the relationship. To Elaine, he represents Theatre. He has the power to advance her.'

'That's just what scares me.'

'I don't see why. He's done well enough by her, up to now. She's had some good notices.'

'Dad, I'm not questioning her ability to perform. But is she using it in the right way?'

I frowned. 'I don't get you.'

Plucking the cherry from her cocktail, Katie ate it lingeringly. 'I hate to sound like Big Sister . . .'

'Don't worry. To me, you still sound like Small Daughter.'

She remained serious. 'I'm determined to say it. Elaine's career, in my view, is sliding in the wrong direction, and I think the Maxwell influence is to blame.'

'What you mean is, she should be getting a solid grounding in repertory, rather than taking lead roles in the London Fringe?'

'There's Fringe,' Katie said primly, 'and there's Fringe. The Maxwell brand might do her no good, in the long run.'

I pushed aside the remnants of my egg mayonnaise. 'Why not?'

'Elaine's limiting herself. She used to be such a good comedienne. All she seems to do now is pant and gasp and take her clothes off. It's not getting her anywhere.'

'It's got her to The Backstage.'

'More of the same,' Katie said dismissively. 'The latest Rick Smythe . . . you can guess what form that'll take.'

I sat gazing at her for a moment. 'Coming from you, my dear,' I said mildly, 'this all strikes me as faintly ironic. What you seem to be saying is, Elaine is exploiting the current moral climate to further her own ends . . .'

'That's exactly what I'm saying.'

'In that case, what are you doing yourself?'

Katie looked thunderstruck. 'What I do is entirely different.'

'In what sense?'

'For heaven's sake. You can't equate literature with the stage.'

'No?'

'Of course not! They're two separate things. Stage business is in the hands of the director: he's king. A writer has a . . . a direct relationship with the reader. Motivations can be explored. There's an underlying serious intent—'

'Come on, Katie. The serious intent behind that first novel of yours was to make a name for yourself, wasn't it?'

'If so, it was to ensure that my work started reaching a wider audience. If an author thinks she has something to say, it's natural she should want as many people as possible to hear it. The only way to achieve that—'

'Is to pour in everything and whip it to a froth. Which,' I said relentlessly, 'is precisely what you did. That is, I thought it was everything, at the time. From what I hear of this new one, I may have to revise my ideas.'

Katie's mouth had set into a perilous shape. 'We seem to

be straying from the point. I'm talking about Elaine and her caperings.'

'Don't they amount to much the same thing? She's chosen a slightly different path from yours, that's all, in putting herself on the map. I can't see that anyone has a right to criticize.'

The cheeks of my senior daughter had turned bright pink. Dropping her spoon, she wrenched a lace-edged handkerchief from her sleeve and blew her nose with vigour. 'If it's rights we're talking about,' she said in a muffled voice, through the linen, 'what moral authority do *you* have? Your function in society can hardly be termed uplifting.'

I felt as if I had been struck in the mouth. 'That,' I said stiffly, 'is possibly a matter of opinion. Without being pompous, I'd suggest that as Editor of a leading national—'

'Oh, it leads all right, that *Planet* of yours. Straight down into the gutter. Face it, Dad. What you're doing isn't newscasting: it's the equivalent of modern pantomime. Sex and sniggers and leggy lovelies. That's the sum total of its nature . . . so what gives you the right to carp about a work of literary imagination?'

'Who's carping? Katie, try not to be absurd. I'm merely defending Elaine from what I view to be a rather unjustified attack on the means she's adopted to . . .'

Momentarily I ran dry. I felt short of breath. Katie's forthright comment had knocked the wind out of me, the more so as it scratched at old scars which I had thought to be healed. I felt both affronted and defensive. 'Since we're on the subject of newspapers,' I continued heatedly, 'you're not forgetting, I hope, the part they've played in getting your name on to the top-sellers list. Not excluding the despised *Planet*, whose disobliging Books Page editor—'

'No need to throw that at me. Did I come to you and beg for a review? I did not. Your critic—'

'He knew you were my daughter. What else did you expect?'

It was a nasty, underhand swipe, the delivery of which I regretted before the final syllable had emerged. For a moment or two Katie sat motionless, staring down at the cutlery. Then, very deliberately, she took her dish of melon cocktail in both hands, rose, leaned across the table and emptied the remaining contents over my forehead.

Juice ran into my eyes and nostrils. A lump or two of fruit bounced down on to my shirt-front. In a carrying voice, Katie said distinctly, 'You're arrogant, did you know that? You think you can tweak the strings on everybody. Well, here's one puppet who won't dance.' Turning, she flounced out of the restaurant.

I sat wiping the deposit from my face and lapels. I felt dazed. It had all happened rather fast. Curious or amused glances were coming my way from nearby tables: I did my best to ignore them. After a discreet lapse of time, a waiter presented himself at my elbow with a clean table-napkin and spoke in a murmur. 'Will Madam be returning, sir, for the main course?'

'Does it damn well look like it?' I snarled. Taking a grip on myself, I engineered a smile in his general direction. 'I think I must be losing my touch as a host. Forget the rest of the meal, will you? Sorry about the mess.'

'Quite all right, Mr Rodgers. The washroom is over there.'

'Thank you.' Rising, I set off with some dignity between the tables, only to be accosted by a dinner-jacketed arm.

'What's up, Peter? Didn't she care for the starter?'

I looked down into the grinning face of Jeremy Hickster, chief gossip columnist of the *Record*. He was presiding over a tableful of assorted faces, male and female, most of them goggle-eyed. Resigned to the inevitable, I summoned a slender smile to send back at him.

'A small family difference. I think I asked for it. End of quote, Jeremy, okay? Now if you'll excuse me, I've some scrubbing up to do.' Broadening the smile to embrace the table, I passed on and put the washroom door firmly between us.

'What do you mean,' demanded Elaine, 'she *left* you?'

'We got into a stupid squabble,' I explained, 'about her brand of literature and mine. I said something inexcusable and she took off in a huff.'

Sitting up in bed, Elaine surveyed me in consternation. 'That's ridiculous. You and Katie at loggerheads?'

'It'll blow over.' I spoke with more assurance than I felt. 'I'll call her tomorrow. You know where she's staying?'

'Not exactly.' Elaine looked and sounded a little shifty. 'But she's bound to be getting in touch with me, either here or at The Peacock. If you want me to give her a message . . .' She placed a cool hand on my wrist. 'For goodness sake, Dad, what was it all about?'

'Moral responsibility.'

'That tells me a lot. What did you *say*?'

I quoted the fatal remark. Elaine scowled, peeped at me, then giggled. 'Melon cocktail down your chin . . . I'd have given worlds to see it. Very naughty, though, of Big Sister, even if she did have justice on her side.'

I shifted position on the edge of the bed. 'What's that supposed to mean?'

'Well, she was right, wasn't she? You're in it for the money, just as much as she is.'

I was careful to allow a pause. A fracas with one daughter in an evening was reprehensible: disagreement with the pair of them would have amounted to wilful damage. 'When you come right down to it,' I replied, having studied the pitfalls and plotted my route accordingly, 'that applies to most of us, wouldn't you say?'

'Not to me.' Elaine smoothed the bedsheet with her fingers, looking superior.

Prepared as I had been for a variety of retorts, this one took me aback. Its complacency refuelled my irritation. 'You don't think so?'

She smiled pityingly. 'I know so. People like me are trying to advance the cause of drama.'

I took a long breath. 'With what purpose?'

'For its own sake, of course. What else?'

'Why should drama need advancing for its own sake? Has it ever made the request?'

'Dad, don't be more of a Philistine than you can help. The stage is important: everyone knows that.'

'To whom? Those making a fat living out of it, perhaps. People like . . .'

'Like Jimmy, you were going to say? For your information, he makes precious little out of it. Anyway, you're not suggesting they should all starve?'

'I do suggest they might pause sometimes to ask themselves whether what they're up to serves the best interests of society.'

'Does that include me?'

'We all have our responsibilities.'

Elaine's expression, I noted with a sinking heart, had acquired a coating of permafrost. After a brief delay she said, 'I'm beginning to see why Katie walked out on you tonight. You're saying the most peculiar things. What's got into you?'

I made a clumsy attempt to pat her bare shoulder, which twitched at the contact. 'Overtiredness, probably. I shouldn't have gone back to the office after the bust-up. I should have come straight home. Take no notice of me, darling, or anything I come out with. I don't mean it.'

'You shouldn't say what you don't mean. As a journalist, you should know it gets you into scrapes.' She slid down between the sheets. 'I'm tired. Switch the light off, will you, as you go out?'

Rising reluctantly, I did as she asked. 'Good night,' I said softly. There was no reply.

As I was closing the door, she spoke again from the darkness. 'You left the hairspray at home again. You could at least go through the motions of making an effort.'

CHAPTER 9

Throughout the next morning I phoned home at half-hourly intervals. Each time, Elaine reported that there had been no word from Katie. At my fifth attempt, she said frostily, 'You don't have to keep ringing, you know. If Katie does call, I'll let her know you're anxious to talk to her.'

'But will she respond?'

'I can't say. Having read Jeremy Hickster in the *Record* this morning, I rather doubt it. Why not choose somewhere less public in future for your family reunions?'

I made a retort that was meant to be flippant, and rang off, feeling a little sick. In the normal way, Elaine would have been warmly sympathetic about the whole wretched affair, but I seemed to have made a thumping success of alienating her as well. As I hung up, Laura entered with a tabloid in her grasp. I gave her an expressionless look.

'I've seen it.'

'Oh. I'd assumed it was one of dear Jeremy's more spiteful inventions.' Discarding the *Record*, she draped herself elegantly along my desk. 'I was wrong?'

'Partly. Something of the kind did occur, though the words attributed to both of us are pure fantasy.' Seizing the newspaper, I hurled it across the room. Then I apologized. 'Maybe you wanted to keep that for posterity?'

'Floor-level suits it better.' Her manner conveyed the consolation that I had been starved of elsewhere. 'Peter, I'm most awfully sorry. I know how you feel about Katie. What went wrong?'

I supplied a brief account. 'It was my fault—I want my head examined. I should have had more regard for Katie's feelings.'

'You're entitled to your views,' Laura observed.

'Not when it's a case of the pot calling the kettle black.'

She frowned. 'Am I missing something?'

Leaping up, I prowled twice around the office. 'What right do I have,' I demanded, coming to rest at the window, 'to accuse either of my children of exploiting life for profit? What am I up to myself, for God's sake?'

The frown lingered. 'That's a bit different, surely.'

'You're repeating my original argument, Laura, word for word. I've been thinking about it, and I've concluded there's no difference whatever. I've absolutely no right to talk. What I'm engaged in here, let's face it, is no more or less than incitement to licentiousness. I do it for cash rewards. And what makes it ten times worse is, I've been doing my damnedest all along to fool myself to the contrary.'

'Peter, I really think you're being a shade hard on yourself . . .'

'But don't you see? I'm a phoney. So God-almighty pleased with myself for rescuing the *Planet* from the scrapheap—and why? So that we can tickle the palates of the dirt-lovers? Oh, I knew it before. We're all conscious of it, aren't we? We kick it down, hold it under the surface while we're getting on with the job. The power of the Press. We only let it mean something when we're trying to sway attitudes. The rest of the time, we pretend it's not there. The whole thing's a sham.'

With a savage kick at the *Record* on the carpet, I returned to the desk and sat heavily. Laura gazed at me in silence.

Presently she said, 'The fact remains, neither Katie nor Elaine should have—'

'They were both fully entitled to turn on me. They love what they do, they want success, so they're blind to the consequences. Just like their father. For Christ's sake, Laura, do you realize—'

She burst into a soprano peal of laughter. Shocked, I sat staring at her. Wiping her eyes with a paper tissue, she turned back to face me, brandishing her free hand to keep me silent. 'I'm not going to allow any more. You know what it's called, Peter? Menopausal self-doubt. The mid-life crisis. Everyone hits it. With you, it's taken this form, and the Katie business has triggered off the symptoms, but I'm buggered if I'm going to sit by and let you flail yourself to ribbons while everyone else simply carries on. Why should you shoulder the sins of the world? You're a mirror: you reflect. No one's asking more of you.'

'Then they should be. Instead of reflecting, why don't I illuminate? I've got the means.'

'You haven't. You know as well as I do, if you tried anything along those lines the *Planet* would fold in a month. What good would that do? As things stand, at least you're able to—'

A double rap on the door, followed by the appearance of Andy Kent, felled her in mid-flight. With a painful effort I winched my mind back to a professional level. ''Morning, Andy. Don't mind us; we're having a semi-philosophical debate and neither of us is winning. Take a seat. Be with you in a minute.

'My cue for departure,' said Laura, smiling at him. 'We'll continue this, Peter, some other time. How about tonight, over a meal? I don't chuck my fruit cocktails around, I promise you.'

'Can't. I'm dining with the Governor.'

'No wonder you're feeling morbid. Later in the week, then.

Give Sir Giles my love, when he gets back from his tour of the estate. You know he does it every evening, six o'clock on the dot? Shakes up his liver, he told me once. You should do something of the sort. Twice around the block, rain or shine . . . does wonders for the mental outlook. Treat him gently, Andy, he's feeling fragile.' With a faintly mocking yet compassionate grin, she fluttered some fingers at me and let herself out of the office. Sagging into my chair, I met the newcomer's diffidently questioning glance with as much aplomb as I could muster.

'She's exaggerating a little. Right, Andy, let's have it. Did you manage to achieve either of the contacts you mentioned?'

Taking out cigarettes, he passed me one, lit up for both of us, resettled himself with a faint sigh of exertion. '*Contacts* would be stretching things. I did contrive a verbal exchange with Paul Lewis's mother, who now dwells in a third-floor flat in Bayswater behind an entryphone system that would give access problems to King Kong. She's turned eccentric. No recollection of me at all; seemed to imagine I'd come to talk about the rent. I tried asking about letters, but I got nowhere.'

'No chance of a peek at her son's correspondence?'

'None left. She's cleared it out, or else it got lost. She was vague about it, but I could hardly take the flat apart to check.'

'Wouldn't have done a lot for our image. How about the widow, Sharon? You've not seen her yet, of course.'

'Yes, I have. Same zero result.'

'Carl Scott, then. You mentioned a brother . . .'

'I'm fixed to meet him this afternoon. This is what I came in to ask. On the assumption that I run into more obstruction, how . . . ah . . . generous can I be? I'm not fully primed yet on *Planet* policy.'

'Keep it under four figures,' I said mechanically, 'unless more seems justified, in which case you'll need special clearance. You might try, first, putting it to him as a matter of public interest. Flog the point that we're trying to prevent further—'

'Naturally.'

'You'll let me know tomorrow how you make out?'

'Tonight, if you like.'

'Not tonight. I'll be in Surrey.'

'Ah yes. Dinner with the Governor.' Andy looked at me with a quirk of the lips. 'One of the managerial perks?'

'If it is,' I said sourly, 'it's a specimen I could do without. A twenty-mile drive for half-cooked beef and a pep talk isn't my idea of jollity.'

'As bad as that? No wonder Sir Giles has to take exercise before he can tackle it. Is that right, what Laura was saying—he tours the estate every evening?'

'Regular as clockwork. But I doubt if exercise has much to do with it: he just likes to know the boundary fences are still in place. Anyhow, Andy, there's no rush. Report to me in the morning, huh?'

'You say there's no rush,' he said meditatively, 'but I'm just wondering about the opposition. The *Record*, in particular. After what they wrote, aren't they likely to be chasing the same . . .'

'I think, Andy, the painstaking approach might be the one to pay off in this case. If the opposition want to stampede around, let 'em. They could miss something.'

He stood up. 'Stately progress, then. No fireworks. I'll liaise tomorrow.' Pausing at the door, he flashed me an evil grin. 'Hope you don't lose any fillings during the main course.'

As I swung the Cavalier between the fluted stone pillars, capped by ceramic minarets, flanking the entrance to the drive that led to the main door of the Governor's Surrey seat, my spirits dropped to sea-level.

It wasn't just the matter of food and drink and shop-talk. My rediscovered mood of self-examination, far from dispersing, seemed to be gaining ground, taking firmer hold, starting to re-tint my attitude towards most of the things I had reasoned myself into accepting in the course of the past couple of years. Feeling as I did, I was not going to find it easy to survive the evening without giving something away. I hoped Sir Giles was not in one of his more perceptive frames of mind.

· There was also the question of the girls. No word had reached me from Katie. From lunchtime onwards, my calls to the apartment had bleeped in vain, Elaine having taken herself off to rehearsal. In desperation I had tried Katie's agent. She had, she informed me, seen her favourite author the previous day and was not expecting her to be in touch again for a while. An obscurely derisive quality had been detectable in her voice. Doubtless she was an avid reader of Jeremy Hickster.

Thus I was left on a prickly footing with both my daughters simultaneously. The situation was, for us, unique, and I didn't like it. I ached to patch things up. The fact that no immediate way of doing so was available added up to frustration of a kind that made me want to accelerate in a sweep at the head of the drive and make off back to central London in a wild bid to track down the pair of them. But I couldn't. I was expected, and here came Stacker from a side door to help haul me out of the car. Before cutting the engine I gave vent to a loud and prolonged groan. It was the last I should be able to indulge in for several hours.

Stacker, boringly, was Colonel Sir Giles Horley's ex-batman, who had remained faithfully in his service to treble-up as footman, butler and jobbing gardener while his wife functioned as cook and housekeeper. Both of them took their duties with a dogged solemnity that was unnerving. Accepting Stacker's muscular forearm, I said as I hit the gravel,

"'Evening, Ron. Governor not back yet, I suppose?'

'Still on his rounds, Mr Rodgers. Keeping all right, sir?'

'I scrape the mould off every morning. Who else have we got tonight?'

'Just the Trenchards, sir, and their daughter. Not met them, have you?'

'No.' I cheered up a little. I had asked more in hope than expectation, but it seemed that I was not to be the only guest. The thing I had dreaded most was a tête-à-tête over brandy and cigars with the Governor after the meal. 'Lively bunch, are they?'

'A very likeable family, sir,' he intoned. 'Quite close neighbours of the Colonel. I think you'll find them agreeable.'

'Bless you, Ron.' I waved to Lady Horley, who had appeared on the main steps of the house. A forthright woman with some military experience of her own, she scorned the conventions and would have greeted me in dungarees and a headscarf had she felt inclined. In this instance she was wearing a woollen two-piece outfit in vivid purple with an immense silver chain about her neck, like a halter; I felt that Stacker should have been leading her reverently into an enclosure for auction. "'Evening, Lois,' I called. 'Am I a little early? Wasn't sure about the traffic, so I left in good time.'

'No need to apologize.' Touching my hand for an instant as I approached, she turned to lead the way indoors. 'Our friends from Down the Road,' she proclaimed, stumping ahead of me into a sitting-room with french windows overlooking the grounds in traditional style, 'are usually the early birds. For them, this is late.'

'Governor keeping well?'

'I've not set eyes on Giles,' she drawled, as if accounting for an unfamiliarity with his condition, 'since four o'clock tea. He went out to inspect the fence-posts on the east perimeter or somewhere, which means he probably won't be back until we're sitting down to the soup. Have something to drink and tell me about Fleet Street.'

'Is that what you'd really like?'

'No,' she returned candidly. 'I'm not in the smallest degree interested. I thought you might like to talk shop.'

'Not this evening, I think.' I met her gaze, which was of the piercing variety. 'I expect you've seen today's *Record*?'

'I've had the Hickster page *displayed* to me.' She glared accusingly at Stacker as he passed us on his way to the drinks trolley. 'The height of bad taste, as always. When is the writ being served?'

'There's no point in suing. Ignoring the embroidery, the core of the item is true.'

She looked disbelieving. 'Tell me.'

With suitable discretion, over a dry martini, I complied, thankful for a conversational topic that would fill the pre-dinner vacuum. Although I half-liked Lady Horley, I never felt at ease in her company and was always glad to be clear of her penetrating inspection. For ten or fifteen minutes she listened attentively; then her gaze started to wander. Several times she puckered her eyes at the brass antique clock on the mantelshelf. Clearly, her interest in the newsworthy behaviour of Katie was evaporating fast. At ten minutes to eight she abandoned all pretence, rose, and moved restlessly to the door.

'Stacker! Any sign of the Trenchards?'

'Not yet, ma'am,' I heard him reply.

'Any sign of Sir Giles?'

'No, ma'am.'

'Go and look for him, will you? Tell him one of his guests is here.'

Feeling that some apology for being there was called for, I said, 'I'm afraid I rather jumped the gun this evening. The traffic . . .'

'Nonsense. Giles should be on hand to entertain his visitors. Will you excuse me for a moment? Do help yourself to another drink.' Looking thunderous, Lady Horley tossed herself through the doorway and vanished in a fusillade of heeltaps on parquet.

On my arrival it had been dusk. It was now dark outside, but for some minutes an occasional lightning flash had been illuminating the sky, thunder was rolling distantly, and the interior lamps threw into relief a pattern of raindrops on the panes of the french windows. Abandoning my martini glass, I went over to the trolley to serve myself with a Scotch. Stacker seemed to have disappeared. Taking the drink to the windows, I stood watching the glimpses of garden revealed to me by the storm. Beyond the lawns, covering perhaps half an acre, most of the Horley estate consisted of woodland, providing what a property agent would have described as total seclusion and what someone of a nervous disposition might have called claustrophobic isolation. Either way, I thought, the Governor was welcome to it. I thought of the apartment, and Elaine. I wished I was back there, chatting to her.

Failing this, I wished Stacker would reappear. I glanced around for a bell-push or something to rattle; there was nothing. Lady Horley had been gone seven minutes. Apart from the thunder and the odd spatter of rain against the glass, no sounds were reaching me. The house seemed to have curled up and expired.

Watch out for yourself, Dad, until this latest maniac is under lock and key . . .

Shaking myself half-angrily, I turned from the window and went out to the hall. Its oak panelling looked back at me with silent indifference. If Lady Horley had ever been around, which I was beginning to question, she had dissolved in a puff of pink smoke. As for Stacker . . .

His wife, I thought, must be in evidence somewhere. Presumably there was a meal to be cooked and served.

Traversing the parquet, I was on the point of releasing the catch of a heavily-carved door that looked as if it might lead to a kitchen area when footsteps rang on the stone steps outside the hall. They sounded hasty. Returning to the main entrance, I was in time to catch a figure as it irrupted squelchily from the porch to an accompaniment of gasps. Hoisting it upright, I stared into the agitated face of a teenage girl.

'Hullo,' I said, with the heartiness of relief. 'Get caught in the storm?'

Shovelling aside rat-tails of sodden hair, she peered up at me bug-eyed. 'Are you Mr Rodgers?'

'That's me. You're Miss Trenchard, am I right? I was just—'

'They asked me to come and find you. Something dreadful's happened.' She puffed for a moment. 'It's Sir Giles.'

'Heart attack?' The words came automatically to my tongue. He had always seemed to me a ripe candidate.

'Worse.' She collapsed on to a chair.

'An accident?'

She nodded, then shook her head with some energy. 'It was horrible. We were on our way here when we found him. I'll never forget it, never.'

Crouching beside her, I said gently, 'Was he hit by a car?'

'He wasn't on the road.' She stared dully ahead. 'The police are there now—you'll have to ask them. But I don't see how it could have been an accident.'

CHAPTER 10

Elaine had coffee and sandwiches waiting. Observing my fatigue, she delayed her interrogation: she had something of her mother's diplomacy at times. When I felt revived, I gave her an edited account of the evening.

'The detail,' I said wryly, 'you'll find in tomorrow's *Planet* exclusive. The syntax may be a little scamped, but I can vouch for the content.'

My position in the course of a fraught couple of hours had been a delicate one, precariously balanced between the roles of on-the-spot reporter, hearsay witness and friend of the family, in which last capacity I had felt morally obliged to offer such comfort as was feasible to Lady Horley in the extremity of her distress. The extent of her disintegration had startled me rather. I had always gained the impression that she cared very little whether her husband continued to function or not. Yet another instance, I reminded myself, of deducing too much from appearances.

By the time I had felt able to leave her to the sedative care of her doctor and the Stackers, three editions of the *Planet* containing my story were on their way to remote corners of the British Isles. In addition, I had dashed off a personal tribute to replace the Comment on local government corruption carried in earlier editions. Between these duties, I had done my best to deal coherently with the inquiries of the Regional Crime Squad team that was infesting the house and grounds, and had been more than thankful for the facilities made available to me on the quiet by the Stackers, whose small converted flat above the stables had, fortuitously, its own telephone on a separate line. It was not until I was driving home that I came out of trauma to face up to the fact that the Governor, poor wretch, had finally succeeded in submitting a valid proposal for a sensation by getting himself slaughtered.

'I did tell you,' Elaine said reasonably, refilling my cup, 'it could happen to anybody. Now will you take precautions?'

'Sir Giles wasn't anybody. He was a loony old bugger who fancied himself as a country squire and managed to antagonize the locals in the process. Quite a few people must have wanted to kill him.'

Elaine snorted. 'What did he do? Have the peasants whipped, and rape their daughters?'

'For one thing, there was trouble over his plan for a sports complex on the edge of his estate. According to the Trenchards—'

'People don't get murdered over things like that.'

'Don't they?'

'It's too coincidental by half. Yet another mugging victim who just happens to be in the entertainment business. If it was simply a local issue, I'll eat that pot-plant.'

'It was hardly a mugging, in the accepted sense,' I demurred, avoiding the main thrust of her argument. 'He was attacked on the edge of his own land, at a time when he was dressed in his tattiest gear and obviously carrying nothing of value.'

'Well, then?' Elaine said triumphantly.

'So there must have been a specific motive. Someone had it in for him.'

'Exactly.'

'Someone,' I said stubbornly, 'from close by.'

'The Trenchards, maybe? You think he'd been carrying on with this daughter of theirs?'

'I think we're leaping to conclusions. Let's wait to hear what the cops find out.'

'And meanwhile, the killer walks around lining up his next target. Whoever he is, he's now got the popular Press in his sights, that's clear. You could be next.'

'So what do you want me to do?' I demanded. 'Claim police protection?'

'That's what they're supposed to be there for.'

'My dear, one has to be practical. The police can hardly be everywhere, guarding every pipsqueak who feels threatened.'

'Can't you take an early holiday?' she urged. 'Go abroad for a month. By the time you get back—'

'Elaine, I admit this has come as a shock, but I see no point in being stampeded. Reasonable precautions are one thing: hysteria is another. I'll go on taking care, I promise.' I drew a couple of breaths. 'And don't lose sight of your own security while you're fixated on mine. Get Jimmy to bring you home every night, if you can. How did it go, this evening? Good audience?'

She stiffened instantly. 'Much as usual,' she said tersely, rising from the sofa. 'If you've finished, I'll take the tray. It's almost one o'clock.'

Manifestly I was far from forgiven. Watching her glumly as she made for the kitchen, I toyed with and then dismissed the idea of asking yet again whether Katie had been in touch. If Elaine had wanted to, she would have told me. The atmosphere was one I was going to have to live with for a while. Feeling depressed, I was tugging at my necktie when Elaine returned.

'I'm off to bed.' Without approaching to be kissed, she headed purposefully for the hallway leading to the bedrooms, paused at the door and glanced back. 'Now that you've lost Sir Giles,' she said on a speculative key, 'what's going to happen to the dear old cuddly *Planet*, I wonder? A switch of direction, or more of the same?'

Understandably, it was one of the first questions to come up at the editorial conference next morning. I guessed that it was the burning issue throughout the building, and I wished I could feel more confidence in my declaration that, to the best of my knowledge, no change in the *Planet*'s status or policy would stem from the death of its chairman. His deputy, Alan Turnbull, would be taking over—we had spoken by telephone the previous evening and early that morning—and the board, I explained, were united in their desire to have things continue as before. Wally Farr, who had raised the matter, betrayed scepticism.

'What if we hit bad times?'

'Suppose we avoid that,' I countered.

'Some things can't be avoided. Recession could flatten us. The Governor would have sweated it out, seen us through. Can we rely on the board doing the same?'

'As you know, Wally, I never place total reliance on anybody or anything. For the moment, I suggest we just plug on, pray for stability. After all,' I pointed out, 'we knew the Governor wasn't immortal. He could have gone any time. Once Turnbull gets himself organized, I'm sure we'll have nothing to worry about.'

Nobody looked consoled.

After the meeting, Laura stayed behind. 'Did you mean that, Peter, about there being no policy switch? Or were you just whistling to keep our spirits up?'

'I see no reason,' I told her, 'for the board not to view things logically. Why change a winning formula?'

She sniffed. 'Some people seem to crave change for its own sake.' She glanced around the room, which had now emptied. 'Perhaps you can tell me something. What exactly was the murder weapon used on the Governor?'

'Why, are you thinking of recommending it to battered wives?'

'I just wondered whether it had been found.'

I shrugged. 'If it has, they're not saying. The Chief Super on the case, guy by the name of Felton, didn't want to tell me much. I got more out of one of the sergeants. A blunt instrument, he said, with masterly originality. Iron crowbar, heavy wrench . . . you name it, they were looking for it.'

'They're guessing,' said Laura.

'Do they ever do anything else?'

'I'm not sure.' She was looking fixedly at Katie's water-colours behind my head. 'It would be interesting to know.'

Her mind seemed to be elsewhere. To fetch her back, and also to provide a gentle hint that I needed my office to myself for a while, I said, 'See you for lunch? I'd like your advice on something.'

Her eyes re-focused. 'Okay, fine,' she said vaguely. 'Make it one-ish, okay?'

When I was alone, I put in a call to the Cotswolds. The telephone in Katie's hideaway bleated obediently for the two minutes I hung on, but nobody picked up the receiver. I gave up. Almost immediately an incoming call came through. The eagerness with which I snatched up the instrument drained away through my feet as the self-esteeming voice of Jeremy Hickster vibrated down the line. I said, 'I wonder you've the gall to talk to me.'

'I'll talk to anybody, you know that. Nothing personal, old man. Just inquisitive to know how you feel this morning.'

'How should I feel?'

'Well, you know. The man at the hub of violence, two nights running . . .'

'Careful, Jeremy. It might get to be a habit.'

'Threats? I take karate lessons, let me tell you. In my profession, it's as well to keep in trim. But seriously, Peter, what next? A murderous assault from a crazed compositor? Do you ever get the feeling—'

'The feeling I'm getting right now,' I interposed, 'is that unless you're off the line before the count of three, something rather devastating will happen to the *Record*'s contingency libel fund, and if you think I'm joking . . . Come in!' I roared in answer to a knock. 'Do I make myself clear?' I asked the receiver. 'Don't push your luck . . . old man.'

'Taut nerves,' Hickster declaimed with relish, 'at Planet House. Shell-shock and tension. Tell me, is it true what I've been hearing about your late Governor? Was he really on the point of flogging the *Planet* to Pinkie Publications and sinking the proceeds in a fun palace at his Surrey seat, right on the spot where he was found? Rumour has it—'

I slammed down the receiver. Andy Kent, who had entered quietly and taken his customary seat at the far side of the desk, eyed the instrument as it quivered. 'Anyone I know?'

'Two guesses,' I growled, leaning back and inhaling. 'You won't be needing the other one. Got something to tell me?'

'This is probably a bad time. I'll look back later and—'

'Later will be worse. Let's get out of this madhouse. Feel like a brandy?'

'At this hour?' Puzzled, he pursued me to the ground floor and a rear exit which took us into a maze of back streets and ultimately to a varnished wooden door at the corner of an inconspicuous red-brick building with a view of Holborn Viaduct. A flight of stairs led to a first-floor room with low-slung cushioned chairs at one end and a minuscule bar at the other. Three or four men and a woman, in two groups, were in occupation. They took no notice of us. An elderly, ravaged bartender served me stoically, without a hint of recognition. I carried the drinks across to Andy, who was looking about him curiously from a seat by the window.

'Open to editors and above,' I explained, dragging up another chair. 'This is the one place hereabouts where I can pull rank and get a bit of peace. I've made a point of keeping up my subscription. You won't believe it, but that barman and I are thoroughly acquainted. He says good morning at Christmas. Right, let's hear what you've got.'

'It's not much. Compared with your experience—'

'Never mind that. Did you see Carl Scott's brother?'

He nodded. 'Took me longer than I'd allowed for. He's moved to Hampshire. I motored down and got lost. Still, when I did finally arrive he was willing to help, though I had a job to make it clear to him just what I was after. He's like most of the others. They've grown accustomed to the idea that the killings were for profit, and Ian Scott's no exception.

Bank official. Logical mind. His brother's study was ransacked, things were taken, ergo . . . The idea of some other motive hadn't occurred to him.'

'But you managed to implant it, in the end?'

'Well, he invited me home—I saw him first at the bank—to take a look at what he'd got of Carl's. A few personal items. One or two bits of correspondence.'

'Nothing helpful?' I asked gloomily.

Andy made no immediate reply. Steadying his brandy glass, he swayed sideways to get a hand at his inside pocket, extracted something, placed it on the arm of my chair. It was a clear plastic bag housing a folded sheet of grimy paper. Noting my hesitation, he said, 'You can take it out.'

Unfolded, the sheet displayed four typewritten paragraphs. Addressed to 'My dear Mr Scott', they were signed at the foot, in block capitals, BYSTANDER. Andy waited while I read down. When he could see that I was going over it again, he said deprecatingly, 'Not that significant, I imagine. I only brought it away because—'

'Hold on.' I completed my re-scrutiny. 'I'm not so sure about that, Andy.'

He scratched his neck. 'Something I've missed?'

'I don't know. To the casual eye, there's not a vast deal in common between this and the note sent to Mel Winters, except that the signature . . .' By now I had produced the Winters letter from my wallet. Spreading it alongside the Scott one, I compared them. Andy leaned across and twisted his neck to do likewise. 'VIEWFINDER,' I said slowly. 'Also typed in capitals. Different machine, admittedly. Anyone can see that.'

'But the two names have a similar ring to them.'

'Just what I thought. Can the same be said of the text? The tone seems to vary. Whereas Winters is described as *a parasite feeding on human frailty*, Scott gets away with a kind of reproachful scolding, as in . . .' I slid a finger down the paragraphs. 'This: *It saddens me to think that fortunes are being coined, quite legally, by the exploitation of society's present tolerance* . . .' I glanced up. 'A marked difference in intensity. When you think about it, though, is the gap really so wide?'

Andy sat back to consider. '"Making money out of dirt." Isn't that what both charges boil down to?'

'Near enough.'

'But showbiz celebrities must be getting crank letters all the time.'

'I'm sure you're right.' I paused. I was thinking of the one that Elaine had shown me. Harmless enough, on the surface. A guileless tribute. The signature on that one had been ink-scrawled, illegible. The typing . . . Thrusting back the recollection, I added, 'They just have to take them in their stride. These two samples, though . . . Anything strike you about them?'

'The construction?'

'Right.' Picking up the sheets, I scanned from one to the other. 'Four paras in each case. The first one, you'll notice, commends the technical competence, if nothing else, of the recipient. The second is the breast-beating bit, warning of the possible dire effects of such expertise. This leads on to—'

'I see what you're getting at. Both third paras take the thesis a stage further by questioning their motives. And finally . . .' Andy peered over my shoulder. 'The punchline in both letters hints at retribution. Identical formula.'

'We could be reading too much into it,' I cautioned. Sliding both sheets into the plastic wrapper, I returned it to my wallet. 'In my eagerness to trace a link, I wouldn't want to incite anyone to manipulate evidence.'

'Heaven forbid.'

'If you can call it evidence. Straws in a light breeze, might be a better description.' I hesitated, then decided to mention it. 'My daughter Elaine received a note quite recently.'

'Oh? In what connection?'

'She's an actress. She's playing at the—'

'I remember reading about her. The avant-garde thing at The Peacock?'

'That's the one. She had this anonymous message, congratulating her on her performance. At least, I think it was.'

Andy looked mystified. 'You think it was anonymous?'

'No—congratulatory. If I can recall the wording . . .' With an effort of memory I quoted it. Andy frowned briefly into space.

'In her position, I think I'd have taken it at face-value. Why not?'

'Couldn't tell you,' I confessed. 'If we hadn't been discussing these others, I doubt if I'd have given it a second thought.'

'It's not a bit the same,' he pointed out.

'Except that the message itself was typewritten.'

'Four people out of six type everything, these days,' he said rallyingly. 'I'd be surprised if your daughter had anything to worry about. This play of hers—is it set for a long run?'

'It closes this week. But she's already in rehearsal for a new one at The Backstage. A Rick Smythe special.'

'I'd be interested to see it.'

'I'm taking Laura Cadey to the first night. If you want to risk it, I can probably wangle a couple more tickets.'

'A single will do.' He said it placidly, but I felt a heel for my lack of finesse. 'How much are the seats?'

I waved a hand. 'Daddy gets them as a Fringe benefit . . . so to speak. Anyhow, Jimmy Maxwell would gladly pay you to come along, I dare say. Help fill the empty rows.'

'Who's Jimmy Maxwell?'

I described him briefly, and was progressing to an account of his slightly bizarre relationship with his leading lady when the clock behind the bar caught my eye. I scrambled up. 'End of interlude. Let's get back. I'm going to hold on to these letters, Andy, for the present. I need to think about 'em.

Do you have any remaining commitments?'

He spread his hands. 'At your service.'

'In the wake of what's just happened, there's an obvious new line of inquiry. I'd sooner not make it myself. Fancy a trip into Surrey?' I slapped him on the shoulder as we started down the stairs. 'You're the man in practice. See how you make out with a grieving widow, very recently bereaved.'

CHAPTER 11

'You won't forget,' I said to Elaine, 'I'd like tickets for the first night?'

'You won't want to bother with it.' The reply was brisk. She picked up the marmalade pot from the table. 'Finished with this?'

'I'm in the market for three.'

'Three what?'

'Seats, of course. I'm bringing our Woman's Page editor, and there's someone else who—'

'Oh gosh. I wouldn't. You won't care for it.'

'I'd prefer to be the judge of that,' I said temperately.

'Have you heard from Katie?'

'You know I haven't. Don't change the subject. I always attend your first nights, don't I? What makes you think I want to duck out of this one?'

'I hadn't given it any thought,' she said loftily. 'Too busy rehearsing.' She vanished back into the kitchen.

I sat smouldering, stuck for something else to say. Presently she reappeared, clad in a scarlet anorak and clutching a plastic bag. 'Need a few basics,' she remarked, heading for the outer door. 'If you're serious about tickets, I'll see what I can do. Can't promise. See you later.'

'Why shouldn't I be—' The clump of the door sliced off the rest of the sentence.

★

'Plenty of fresh stuff coming along,' Wally Farr said in a satisfied way. 'Before I tell you about it, what's the position as regards Andy Kent and his solo mission? Anything I should know of?'

'Not yet.' I closed the sliding door of his cubicle so that the aural distractions of the newsroom were blocked out. 'If anything does break, I'll see you get notice.'

'Fair enough. We'll chase up the rest of it, see how it pans out.'

'How's the manpower shortage?'

'Nothing desperate.'

'Only I'd like to monopolise Andy a little longer, if it's okay by you.'

'Sure. No problem.'

'I just have this feeling that if I call him off too soon, I may regret it. Don't ask me why.'

'I wasn't planning to.' His gaze loitered in my direction. To evade it, I picked up a handful of proofs and thumbed through them. After a moment he said, 'You sound pre-occupied. Bad news from the board?'

'None that I know of.'

'That's a relief.' Again he hesitated. 'Something up, then, on the personal front? Is the job starting to get to you?'

Wally and I had known one another a long time. His acuteness came as no surprise, but I wasn't sure how to deal with it. I took a few seconds over my reply.

'Maybe I'm just trying to think a little more deeply about things. This business of the Governor came as a shock.'

'Too right it did. But I don't see why that should affect your approach to journalism.'

I glanced up from the proofs. 'Has it?'

'I don't know, Peter. You tell me.'

I stared out through the glazed partition. At their desks, reporters were typing, telephoning, consulting. Smoking, gesticulating, frowning in quest of a phrase. Nothing had altered. Nothing I could put into words. As it was Wally, however, I tried.

'Perhaps you're right. Probably I do feel a little differently about certain aspects of the job. Tightening up my approach. Something like that.'

'Useful trend,' he said consideringly, 'up to a point.'

'As long as I don't get cramp under it, you mean?'

His mouth gave a twitch. 'We do have the real, harsh world of commerce to contend with. As you're always reminding me.'

'Could it be that it's a world we've helped to create?'

Wally released a hollow groan. 'That clinches the diagnosis. You're suffering a bad attack of the scruples.'

'Self-doubt.'

'Call it what you like. The sentiment does you nothing but credit, my old chum, and it'll bring you down in flames. You can't have it both ways. The *Planet* is what it is: the reading public, bless 'em, are what they are. Either you accept it, or you quit. There's no middle course.'

'That's pretty cynical.'

'It's reality. If you want to preach, climb into a dog-collar. If you want those people out there to keep their jobs, just follow your brief and watch the life-blood continue to flow. Take your pick.'

'You know, Wally,' I said after a lengthy interval, 'there's no one else in this building I'd have taken that from.'

His face split into a grin. 'There's no one else I'd have bothered to sling it at.'

I told Andy to come in and shut the door. Dropping into his usual chair, he waited patiently for me to finish reading the Press clipping I had in my fingers. Presently, with a sigh, I let it flutter down on to the desk.

'I'm calling it off,' I said abruptly.

He didn't blink. On a note of semi-apology I added, 'The effort isn't justified. After the blank you drew yesterday with Lady Horley and the Governor's files, we've nowhere else to go. To get anywhere, we'd need to do a saturation job on virtually everyone who might at some time have received fishy letters through the post, and we haven't the resources.'

Andy nodded. 'I can see that.'

'In the meantime, although Wally Farr says he can cope with the staff he's got available, I've a feeling he wouldn't turn away some extra help.'

'So you'd like me to report to him for duty?'

'I think so.' With the decision made, I felt more light-hearted. 'Thanks for all you've done on this. Sorry it didn't lead to anything.'

'That's the way it goes,' he said cheerfully. On the point of rising, he sank back. 'In my spare time, I might go on seeing one or two other people on the offchance of a breakthrough. Any objection?'

'None, provided your other assignments don't suffer. Before you go, Andy . . . While you were down at the Horley place yesterday, you didn't pick up any more, off the record, about the Governor's death? The murder weapon, for instance. No new leads?'

'I did have a word with an inspector on the team. According to him, they now favour the theory that it was someone who drove along in a vehicle, parked somewhere in the neighbourhood, took a wheelbrace or a spanner with him to the Governor's boundary fence and lay in wait till he came by.'

'That implies it was someone who knew his habits.'

'Plenty of people did, by all accounts.'

'The locals, you mean? And they're the ones who were going to be affected by this fun-palace scheme of his. Hm. So all they're looking for now,' I observed, 'is an anonymous vehicle with a bloodstained tool packed under the spare wheel. Shouldn't take them more than twenty years.'

Andy said ironically, 'Miracles can occur.'

The tone of voice of Katie's agent was more aunt-like than ever. 'She's asked to be incommunicado for a week or two, Mr Rodgers. As you know, she likes to be able to rest completely after finishing a book.'

'I'm her father, not a tax inspector.'

'I'm sorry. I couldn't tell you where she is if I wanted to—I don't know myself.'

Slowly I restocked my lungs, counting to five. 'She'll be returning to the Cotswolds, in due course?'

'I'm not familiar with her immediate plans.'

'Suppose,' I asked, 'I were a publisher, calling you with a half-million-quid offer for paperback rights? You'd be unable to consult Katie for a fortnight?'

'You're not a publisher,' she said sweetly. 'You're Katie's father. And paperback rights are already tied up. Not,' she added hurriedly, 'for anything like half a million. I'd rather no mention was made of it yet.'

'Don't worry. I can be as uninformative as the best.'

With the receiver still vibrating at my elbow, I dragged notepaper out of a drawer and in the course of the next half-hour, between interruptions, wrote Katie a concise but ingratiating letter. I was a stuffed shirt, I told her, and a hypocrite. Instead of cold fruit cocktail, it should have been hot soup. If she didn't feel like getting in touch, I fully understood; but the door was always open. I sent my fondest love and signed myself Dad, Idiot, Grade A and Penitent's Bar. Without re-reading it, for fear of second thoughts, I sealed it in a Planet House envelope, addressed it after some hesitation to the Cotswolds cottage and sent it down for mailing. For the rest of the day I felt marginally better about things, although I knew that little had really been achieved. It was just a relief to have set things down on paper. If the scribble never reached her, something else would have to be tried.

When I reached home, somewhat earlier than usual because for once everything had gone to plan and we had coasted up to the first edition without fuss, I found mail from the second delivery still lying on the doormat. Elaine, I concluded, had gone off early to rehearsal and was not yet back. Collecting the letters, I went through to the living-room and laid them on the cabinet while I poured myself a large Scotch. I wasn't sure what I was celebrating. Perhaps a slightly less tormented state of mind: no more. It would have been nicer if Elaine had been there.

By the next morning, I thought, she might be over the worst of her pique. There was no real basis for the supposition, except that I was feeling about ten per cent less pessimistic over life in general. Switching on the stereo, I hummed to the opening bars of Grieg's *Peer Gynt* Suite while transporting my drink and the mail over to the couch. Luxuriously at full length, I ripped apart the topmost envelope, an invitation to renew a credit card, and threw it on the carpet. The one beneath it was an offer of wine by the case at a discount from a City importer. I discarded this too.

The third contained a brief personal note from Lady Horley, thanking me for the *Planet*'s sympathetic coverage of the Governor's extinction and hoping that our Mr Andrew Kent had been given every possible assistance by herself and the Stackers in the course of his very discreetly-conducted inquiries, which she fervently hoped might yield something of value to the authorities. With a renewed sense of faint guilt, and feeling sorry for her, I placed it aside for a careful answer later, and slit the fourth and last envelope.

The typeface on the single sheet of notepaper seized my eye at once. There was a similar tendency for the capitals to hover. The 'a's' and 'e's' were solid instead of hollow, and the left-hand margin was uneven where the indentation had now and then slipped a character.

Equally redolent was the text itself. Tribute was paid in the opening paragraph to the high standard of my professional accomplishment. In the second, doubt was expressed as to whether I was conscious or not of abusing my undeniable talent to the detriment of several million of my fellow-creatures: the third suggested that the point was perhaps immaterial to me as long as I was able to afford a penthouse apartment near the centre of London and dine at the best establishments.

The fourth and final paragraph, a single sentence, was underscored. The advice it offered was that I should stay on my guard for the foreseeable future, pending a return to quieter times.

The letter was signed, in typed block capitals, CENSOR.

CHAPTER 12

'You say it compares,' said Andy, squinting more closely, 'with the note your daughter was handed at The Peacock?'

'Not in content, but the typeface, certainly. Elaine's kept hers, and I managed to sneak a look at it last night, before she got home. I'm sure it was typed on the same machine.'

He went on scowling over the sheet. I added tentatively, 'Think I'm reading too much into it?'

'In the circumstances, I think it might be unwise to read nothing into it. You know something?'

'What?'

'It's a typeface that's remarkably similar—in fact it's identical—to that on a make of portable that I've just got rid of. A rather offbeat model from a firm called Laski. They went bust. The loops and curls on the capital letters are the same. No mistaking them.'

'A Laski portable,' I said, my interest aroused. 'That could be useful.'

Andy returned the sheet. 'Have you shown this to the cops?'

'No. What can they do? Except spread the word, and that would mean it might get back to Elaine . . . which is the last thing I want. She's paranoiac on my behalf already.'

He regarded me shrewdly. 'But you do plan some kind of action?'

Returning his gaze thoughtfully, I said, 'What's your workload, at this minute?'

'I'm seeing Gil Purvis a little later on. I'll know more after that, but I understand we're to share an assignment . . .'

'Forget it. Help out here and there, by all means, but I want you available. I'll square it with Wally Farr. Okay by you?'

He chuckled. 'I'm still the new boy around here, remember. I just take orders.'

'At ease, soldier. Everything here is done on a democratic basis. The only reason I'm currently throwing my weight around is that I don't want to pass up what could turn out to be a golden opportunity. If we can—'

Laura's head appeared around the door. ''Morning, you secret pair. Plotting, as usual? Sorry to encroach, Peter, but Meg and I were just wondering about that piece of hers that's still on ice. Can we unfreeze it yet?'

'Not for a day or two,' I told her. 'It hasn't been forgotten, tell Meg.'

'Right.' Tossing Andy a smile, she withdrew and then instantly came back. 'This new play of Elaine's—first night Thursday week, correct?'

'I believe so. You'd still like to see it?'

'You bet.'

'Elaine's seeing about the tickets,' I said uncomfortably. 'Should be no problem.'

'Super.' Laura vanished for good.

I sat doodling on my blotter. Presently I drifted back to awareness of my surroundings. 'If you're still interested,' I said to Andy, waiting patiently with folded arms, 'I'll try for the extra seat, as promised.'

'Very good of you.'

'Actually, you'll be doing me the favour. I want you along anyway, as part of your personal assignment.'

He considered the announcement. 'As review back-up?' he speculated.

'As protection.'

'Ah.'

'Sheer funk,' I explained, 'on my part. No, that's not quite true. It's not the sole reason I'm calling on you. The point is, Andy, I believe we may have a chance here to achieve something dramatic. An exclusive to end 'em all. *Planet Team Nets Maniac*. Sounds good?'

'Sounds fabulous,' he acknowledged cautiously. 'You do appreciate what you could be taking on?'

I shook my head. 'No idea. Apart from anything else, I'm finding it hard to decide whether I'm in deadlier danger now than I was before, or less. How long have I been on the short-list? That's the key question.' I gazed unseeingly across the room. 'Forewarned,' I added presently, 'is supposed to be forearmed, though quite often I take leave to doubt it. As far as it goes, that's the plus factor.'

'And the minus?'

'I'm scared out of my wits.'

'One thought does nag at me,' Andy remarked, ending a cogitative silence. 'Weeks or months could elapse before a possible attempt on your, hum, wellbeing. The suspense could become a little . . .'

'Obviously. That's no doubt what he's after. Which is why I intend to pre-empt him, if possible.'

'How?'

Seizing a notepad, I pondered briefly before beginning to scribble. While I was at it, the telephone blurted twice; Andy answered each time, adroitly diverting the inquiry. Completing my draft, I ripped off the sheet and passed it to him. He scanned it blankly.

'Sorry if I'm retarded, but . . .'

'We run that tomorrow, in bold face on the Gossip page, right? Also we offer it round. Hickster should take it. Anything that looks like taking me down a peg or two ought to appeal to him. You'll see I've fixed it for three days' time. That should give Censor the chance to spot it and make his plans . . . assuming he's a mind to. It's a wild card. He may not even see it. If he does, he may well ignore it. All the same, I figure it's worth a throw.' Sitting back unguardedly, I struck the steel stem of the lampholder behind the chair with the back of my head. Wincing, I massaged the tender part of the scalp. 'If I don't knock myself silly first. What do you say, Andy? Am I being unrealistically hopeful, or just plain starry-eyed?'

Slowly he shook his head, still conning my scrawl. 'On the contrary, I think you might be cold-bloodedly sticking your neck out. But then again, if it did stand the remotest chance of speeding things up a little . . .'

'My view entirely,' I said, and asked him to get it copy-typed before I could change my mind.

At midday I was summoned to the office of the acting Governor, Alan Turnbull.

'Just to confirm, Peter, that the board and I consider you're doing a terrific job and we're right behind you, one thousand per cent. Nothing's been altered by Sir Giles's death. Except possibly . . .'

Here it came. 'Except?' I prompted, on a note of fortitude.

He rolled a knowing smile in my direction. 'Relax, fellah. I'm not about to revoke. Far from it. We've discussed the entire question, the board and myself . . .'

A small-built man of around sixty, with a dried-up manner that suited his dried-up physical appearance, he spoke as if his fellow-directors had remained at the boardroom table in a state of moribundity that would be terminated only when he chose to return to them and activate switches.

'The conclusion we've reached,' he resumed, after a reflective pause, 'is that any shackles you may still have felt to be clanking around your ankles can now be shaken off. From here on, any limbs you feel like going out on are fine by us. Not that you've lacked rope, as it is: we realize that. It's just that, in future, we'd like you to feel free to spread your wings, any way you want.' He peered at me with a glint in his pale blue eyes. 'You read me?'

Notwithstanding the prolificity of his metaphors, the gist was plain enough. I assured him that I had not misunderstood. 'I'm grateful,' I added, 'for the clarification, because there has been a measure of insecurity among my colleagues since the . . . disaster.'

'They thought we'd run scared?'

'Editorial policy,' I said with candour, 'can change.'

'Don't let it bother you. None of us is in the business of slaughtering the goose that lays the platinum egg.' Never a man to leave a perfectly respectable saying alone, Turnbull sat looking pleased with himself, savouring his adaptation, before peering at me again. 'How's that daughter of yours coming along in rehearsal?'

I glanced back in surprise. 'You've heard she's in a new production? She's coping all right, I think. I've not seen much of her lately.'

'The new Rick Smythe, isn't it?'

'That's right.'

'Know anything about it?'

'Only that it's fairly vintage Smythe. Tortured sex, nudity, flagellation . . . the works.'

He gave a birdlike, satisfied nod. 'Doing anything on it?'

'We'll be giving it a notice, of course.'

'Nothing in advance?'

I said cautiously, 'How do you mean?'

His tongue slid across his lips. 'Look, Peter, in case you'd been feeling inhibited—forget she's your daughter, okay? As far as I can see, this is a major new work by a leading playwright of the revolutionary school, and we should treat it as such. A pre-production splash, with pictures: how does that grab you?'

'Could be a winner, I suppose, but—'

'But you didn't like to suggest it because of the family connection. Well, I'm here to tell you that no accusation of nepotism will come your way, should you decide on a sneak preview. In fact, what I'm suggesting is tantamount to an instruction, if you'll forgive the term. An illustrated centre-fold—that's what it cries out for. She's not over-sensitive, I imagine, your daughter?'

'If she is, she's hidden it skilfully up to now.'

'Bit of an eyeful, I'm told. Spends more time out of costume, I dare say, than in?'

'If past form is anything to go by.' I didn't respond to his smirk. Illogically, I felt sickened by it. To me, at this instant, he was not acting Governor of the *Planet*: he was simply a rather objectionable little man making a leering sugges-tion, and I had to fight to keep my hackles down. 'All the same, she insists it's a humdinger of a part, so who am I to argue?'

'You've another daughter, haven't you? Writes books.'

I admitted the felony. 'Actually she's written one book, and there's another on the—'

'Talented family,' he remarked, dismissing Katie to the sidelines where she belonged. 'You'll get that fixed up, then? No holds barred, remember. Assuming the director is ready to string along . . . who is directing, by the way?'

I told him about Jimmy Maxwell. 'I'm sure he'd welcome some advance publicity.'

'Good.' Turnbull rubbed his hands together, in the manner of one essaying a spot of ham acting on his own account. 'I'll look forward to seeing the result. Wouldn't have minded attending a rehearsal myself. But my wife . . .' The rueful gesture of an arm reminded me of what I had heard about his large, domineering spouse who never wanted to go places, and I felt a touch of sympathy for the man; though not much.

Before leaving, I asked Wally Farr to ensure that all editions carried the gossip item I had composed. At sight of it he had twitched his jaw, but he made no comment. A check of the first edition of the *Record* had shown me that Jeremy Hickster, to whom a duplicate of the item had been despatched, had obliged by giving it prominence on the centre-right of his page, painstakingly reworded but accurate in essence. There it was, then. For the moment I could do no more, except to wonder how Katie would react when she read the piece. If she read it. On one level, it didn't really matter whether she did or not; but I couldn't help fostering a hope.

CHAPTER 13

Laura was with me in the office at noon the following day when I received Katie's message. It came to me via her agent, who sounded as though she were reading from a prepared script.

'Your daughter asked me to telephone, Mr Rodgers. She would like me to let you know that she has seen the items in this morning's Press and understands the situation, but feels that in the circumstances the time is not appropriate for what has been suggested, and therefore—'

'She won't be turning up,' I finished for her, tersely.

'She does have other commitments that evening. A foreign rights agent . . .'

'I wouldn't want to damage her other commitments. Perhaps you'll convey my thanks to her for letting me know.'

'I'll do that.'

'No point in inquiring, I suppose, where she is at present?'

'I still honestly don't know.'

'How did this message reach you, then?'

'She just gave me a call. I didn't ask where from.'

'If she comes through again,' I said gruffly, 'perhaps you wouldn't mind giving her my love.'

Cradling the receiver before she could start to negotiate, I sat back and recaptured Laura's gaze, which had been roving tactfully while I spoke. 'Word from Katie,' I said, on a note of faint challenge. 'Peace feelers rejected. No capitulation.'

'Give her a little more time,' she advised. 'It's early days. She may feel that the mode of communication . . .'

'Was a trifle melodramatic? Maybe, but what else could I do? If Katie's bent on keeping out of my sight, she'll have to expect other forms of approach. She knows my methods.'

From her perch on the desk, Laura squinted down at me. 'So, what now? Will you stick to your side of this highly-publicized appointment?'

'Why not?' I flung her a short-lived grin. 'Women have been known to change their minds. I'll be there. I'd look pretty silly if I welshed on what's appeared in cold print in my own newspaper.'

'Considering,' she remarked mildly, 'that you were the one to get melon in your ears, I'd have thought you were the one who was owed the approaches.'

'You don't know what I said to her.'

'It can't have been that bad.'

'As far as Katie's self-esteem is concerned, it couldn't have been worse. And by God, Laura . . .' I slammed the desk with my fist. 'It was so damnably unpremeditated. How do these things come to slip out?'

'The miracle is that so many of them stay in.'

'You're no help. One breakout is too many. It means I wasn't thinking, which is unforgiveable. If anyone should be conscious of the power of ill-chosen words . . .'

'You're being remarkably tough on yourself, Peter.' Rising, Laura made briskly for the door. 'But you may be right in keeping that appointment. As you say, us women do have changes of heart. Katie could be just testing you out. Had you thought of that?'

'I've thought of everything.'

With the door handle at her fingertips, she paused again, eyed me across a shoulder. 'Personally, I think it was plucky of you to have that item inserted. I'm sure she'll appreciate that, on reflection.'

Nobody, I thought wryly, could fully conceive the intrepidity of the venture. In the wake of Laura's departure I picked up that morning's final edition of the *Planet*, already folded to the gossip page, and ran my eye yet again over the piece, like somebody scratching at an itching scab. I knew it by heart, and yet I still wanted reassurance that I had phrased it as well as I could.

Grieved over the recent rift with his elder daughter, best-selling authoress Katie, the Editor of the *Planet* has opted for bold action to put things right.

Peter Rodgers has today chosen this column in his own newspaper to extend an olive-branch to Katie, whose second blockbuster novel, *Tumult*, is understood to be on its way to her publisher.

He wants her to meet him at the scene of their fracas last week—The Gourmet Platter in Chelsea, from which he was last seen staggering with traces of a well-aimed melon cocktail trickling between his eyes. Same day, same time, he wants her to know. Should she decide to relent and turn up, a good meal and a lot of affectionate remorse will await her.

And if she doesn't? 'It's Katie's decision entirely,' says Peter. 'I asked for what I got—she was fully entitled to take umbrage. But I'm hoping she'll give me this chance to make amends. Whatever happens, I'll be there.'

Katie's response, I knew already. It had come as no surprise. In any case, the item had not been addressed primarily to her.

At mid-afternoon I had a visit from Chief Inspector William Harris, one of the murder team investigating the Governor's death.

A chubby-faced man of about forty, he declined all offers of refreshment and came directly to the point. 'On your way to Sir Giles's home that evening,' he asked, ballpoint poised, 'which way did you approach, do you recall?'

'My memory isn't that tattered, Chief Inspector. I drove from the Weybridge direction. It's slightly further but less—'

'Did you pass the Oakhurst Hotel?'

I pondered. 'The big place with a motel attached, by the roundabout? Yes: I remember noticing the cars parked outside. There was a—'

'So from there, you'd have taken the forest route direct to the Horley residence?' Whipping a map from an inside pocket, he spread it on the desk between us. 'Along . . . here.' His index finger stabbed.

I nodded. 'That's the road.'

'Notice anything, while driving?'

'Such as?'

'Anything at all,' he said mysteriously.

I shrugged. 'A lot of trees.'

'Nothing among them?'

'The odd house. I wasn't taking special notice. Why?'

'Besides the dwellings,' he persisted, 'as you approached the Horley place, you didn't happen to spot anything else?'

'Like a marauder, you mean, swinging a crowbar? Sorry.'

'What about vehicles?'

'Oh, there was traffic. At times it was—'

'I'm not talking about the stuff on the road. Did you see anything stationary, parked off the highway?'

I looked at him. 'You've got something specific in mind?'

'A car,' he said with reluctance.

'Any particular variety?'

'Medium size saloon or hatchback. Possibly white, or cream.'

'Can't say I did. Should I have?'

'We've had a report,' he said heavily, with the air of a man bending regulations in the interests of expediency, 'of a vehicle of this general description having been sighted at about six o'clock that evening, parked in a clearing about twenty yards off the road with its nose into some bushes. Nobody in the area lays claim to it.' He screwed up his eyes at me. 'It occurred to us that you might have seen it, too.'

'I came along after seven,' I reminded him. 'Who did spot it?'

'A lad from a nearby cottage. He was walking his dog in the forest when he came across it. Sad to say, he doesn't take much interest in cars. Couldn't identify make or model. He did idly notice the number, but can't recall it in full. Thinks it might have included an S and a W. Can't be positive.'

'Would the car have been visible from the road?'

'Not very,' the Chief Inspector conceded. 'The track leads into the clearing at an angle. In high summer, the foliage would probably have hidden it altogether.'

After some meditation I said, 'If there's a connection, it

seems a bit fragile. How far is the clearing from Sir Giles's house?'

'About half a mile. The car and its owner may have been perfectly innocent, sir, we grant that. But we have to check.'

'On the assumption, I take it, that the killer may have parked there, made off on foot through the trees to the Horley place, attacked Sir Giles, then strolled back and driven off? Makes it all sound rather premeditated.'

Chief Inspector Harris offered no comment. Rising, he buttoned himself back into his coat. 'Grateful for your time, Mr Rodgers. Should you recall anything that might be significant . . .'

'I'll get in touch, naturally.' I saw him out of the door. 'Best of luck with your inquiries.'

'We'll need it,' he said predictably.

After he had gone I sat in thought for a while, before buzzing Andy and asking him to step along. While I was waiting, an outside call came through. Picking up the phone, I said 'Rodgers.'

In reply, my ear was assailed by a muffled cacophony of hammering, whistling, heavy treads, and what sounded like electronic music being relayed over ill-tuned loudspeakers inside an abattoir to an accompaniment of animal bellows. Against the racket, some form of human utterance was just audible. More loudly, I said, 'Can you speak up?'

'Jimmy Maxwell. I'm calling about the . . .' Swallowed up by the rival decibels, the voice again lost all definition. With a sigh, I switched the receiver to my other ear. It was no better.

'I can't make out a word you're saying. Can you try from another—'

Abruptly there was silence, as though a door had been slammed. The distinctive, scissored voice of Maxwell said, 'Hear me now?'

'Clearly. How are you, Jimmy? Rehearsals going well?'

'Shaping up. I'm told you're planning a feature on us?'

'I gather from that, our man's been in touch with you. Has he fixed a night to come and see you?'

'Friday.' Maxwell sounded pleased but a little anxious. 'Can you say when the article's due to appear?'

I consulted my desk calendar. 'Production opens on Thursday week, right? So I would think we'd aim to carry the preliminary spread the day before, or possibly on the Tuesday. My features editor—'

'I only asked,' Maxwell said with apparent ingenuousness, 'so as to know if there'd be time to photocopy it and put it around a bit. That sort of pre-publicity can be helpful, in the right places.'

I allowed a pause. 'Ticket sales not too sprightly?' I asked.

'Could be better.'

'What if I invited our features man to go for Monday, instead?'

'Fine by us,' the director said restrainedly. 'Thanks a lot.'

'Our pleasure. Speaking of tickets,' I added, striking while the iron glowed hot, 'I did ask Elaine to arrange some for me. Would you happen to know whether she—'

'I'll see you get them. Thanks again, Peter. 'Bye now.'

For a raucous instant the noise rushed back, to be extinguished as the line went dead. I was still holding the receiver when Andy put in an appearance. Lowering the instrument, I brandished him into his chair. 'Katie,' I informed him, 'has turned me down.'

'Too bad.'

'On the more crucial level, it'll make things easier. Unless she has womanly second thoughts and decides to show up, after all.'

'Is that likely?'

I shrugged. 'Knowing my daughter, I'd say she'll let me sweat for a while longer. In the meantime, can we run through the arrangements? I'd like to have it all cut and dried. You're acquainted with The Gourmet Platter?'

'Been there a couple of times. Up a side street, behind the King's Road.'

'A badly-lit side street. Close to an alleyway that's practically in darkness. I took a short cut through it a few weeks ago—before all this started to happen—and believe me, it's a cinch for an ambush. Might have been created for the purpose. All right so far?'

'Rhapsodic,' he said sardonically.

'The risk,' I reminded him, 'is going to be run exclusively by me. Nobody else.'

'Thanks a heap. Assuming he's read your piece, you think Censor is going to oblige?'

'If we knew that, we could make things a lot easier for ourselves. Now, here's a rough plan I've drawn of the street layout. What I propose is this . . .'

After we had finalized a procedure of sorts, Andy sat scratching the side of his neck with rhythmic strokes of a capped ballpoint. 'When I joined the *Planet*,' he murmured eventually, 'assignments like this weren't entirely what I had in mind. But I suppose it might make copy, even yet. As long as one of us is alive to write it.'

'At least we're prepared . . . which is more than the others were.'

'Prepared for what?'

Ignoring the query, I said, 'On an allied subject, you wouldn't by chance know anything of the Governor's circle of acquaintances that nobody else does? You had a reputation in the agency, I know, for picking up this and that.'

'What's in your mind?' he asked gingerly.

I told him about the visit from Chief Inspector Harris. 'It's a long shot, but if we knew of anyone—business contact, commercial rival, personal adversary . . . anyone who might have had it in for him in some way—who runs a cream or white medium-car, we might stun the police by handing them some useful information. Anybody occur to you?'

Having glared for a time at the opposite wall, Andy shook his head. 'If it had been a purple double-decker bus with diagonal yellow stripes . . . But a white saloon. They're not serious? If it was there at all—and presumably there's only this lad's word—it could have belonged to anyone of a million motorists.'

'Quite. Anyhow we may know by tomorrow. With the Chief Inspector's permission,' I explained, 'we're splashing on it. *Police Seek Mystery Car in Hunt for Killer.* The owner may come forward as a result. On the other hand, he may not.'

CHAPTER 14

At Laura's invitation, I dined with her that evening at her home in Islington.

She had left the disposal of the Woman's Page to Meg Saunders; I had left everything else to Wally Farr. Confident that tomorrow's *Planet* was in safe hands, I escorted Laura down to the basement garage where we engaged in a mild squabble over who was to drive whom. The notion of taking both cars offended Laura's thrifty streak, and besides, she said, if I was coming anyway, it was nicer to travel together and have the extra time to talk. 'I'll come in yours,' she decided, 'and leave mine here overnight.'

'How will you get here tomorrow?'

'I'll cadge a lift from Andy. He lives not far from me.'

'Maybe,' I said, holding the door for her, 'we should always travel in pairs, these days. Or rather, nights.'

Her dark, watchful eyes subjected me to photo-analysis. 'You could have a point.'

As I drove through the barrier, waved on and saluted by the attendant, she added, 'Alternatively, you've been reading too many of your own Comments. Most of us still seem able to get around without meeting a sticky end.'

'Tell that to the Governor.'

'He copped it in the depths of Surrey.'

'I'm sure that was a consolation.'

'One has to admit,' she said presently, frowning out at the pavement activity, 'big cities nowadays leave something to be desired on the part of pedestrians—if they're unlucky, that is. But surely, inside a car . . . ?'

'Breakdowns have been known to occur. When they do, the stranded driver can be more vulnerable than a walker.'

She glanced at me curiously. 'I never knew you were one for meeting trouble less than half way. Don't tell me you've succumbed to your own propaganda.'

'If so, I'm evidently in a minority of one.'

'You're wrong, you know,' she said unexpectedly. 'A little while back, it may startle you to learn, I joined a self-defence evening class.'

'I don't believe it.'

'Try harder. Us divorcees, living alone, we're easy meat. We have to cater for our own protection. Besides, I thought it might make something to write about for the page. But I soon ditched that idea.'

'Why?'

'The week after I started, Diane Plummer on the *Record* carried a piece on the identical theme.'

'Typical.' Taking some traffic lights on the amber, I dodged around a bus and restored my attention to her. 'Did you get far?'

'What?'

'Along the road to self-defence. You'll be telling me next you're a karate black belt, fourth Dan.'

'It wasn't karate. Just a few holds and throws. Did I get far? I'm not sure,' she said thoughtfully. 'I used to inflict all kinds of damage on my classmates, but then they were flabby little creatures, the lot of them.'

'Hardly a real test.'

'On the other hand, I did give our male instructor one or two nasty falls. He said I was about the strongest female he'd ever come up against and he hadn't been expecting it. Does that make you feel more secure?'

'Less. Keep your hands under your seat-belt, where I can see them.'

Half a mile on, I said exploratively, 'I expect you wish Gerald were at home with you, at times.'

'I do miss him, I suppose. Not as much as I should, perhaps. One can acquire a taste for the solitary existence. Ghastly, isn't it?'

'You wouldn't want Lionel back, then?'

Another street or two went by before she answered, on a low note that hinted at inner tension. 'Lionel finished me for the opposite sex.' After a further pause she added, more normally, 'With a handful of honourable exceptions, needless to say.'

'I'll take that as reassurance.'

'Don't assume too much. Bear right here, it's quicker.'

Laura's house was a wafer-thin, three-storey edifice of charred redbrick in a restored terrace which had been part of a reclamation scheme for the area, property values having soared accordingly since completion. Everything inside, from the lobby onwards, was on a miniature scale, and instantly captivating. The living-room at the rear looked out upon a plant-infested patio encircled by a high wall, and deep-sprung chairs with vivid cushions seemed to be everywhere. After pouring a couple of Scotches, Laura spent ten minutes alone in her Lilliputian kitchen to produce, apparently by a miracle, a meal of cold meats and salad and cherry-topped cheesecake that would have graced the Ritz. We ate from trays on our knees, exchanging desultory remarks, swigging white wine from the bottle she had un-corked. It was a lazy, free-and-easy, infinitely satisfying way of passing an hour in eating and drinking. At the end of it, patting a bulging stomach, I said sleepily, 'You're wasted, Laura, in Planet House. You should be pampering the rich and famous. Influencing destinies.'

'I can do that where I am.'

'In a limited way. I'm talking about—'

'I don't know that it's so limited.' Wineglass in hand, she was sprawled in her chair and gazing reflectively at the ceiling, enunciating a little more carefully than usual. She had accounted for more of the bottle than I had. 'When it comes to influence, you'd have a job to find anything to beat the popular Press, don't you think?'

'Television,' I suggested.

'Mm. On the wane a little, I'd say. Lots of impact still, in brief hammer-blows, but for long-term guidance or reflection of mass attitudes . . .' She brandished the wineglass languidly above her head. 'Fleet Street still reigns supreme, in my opinion.'

I gave solemn consideration to the premise. 'On that basis,' I inquired, 'how good a job would you say we do?'

'We? The *Planet*?' Recrossing her legs, she gave a heave of the shoulders. 'Variable.'

'As a matter of interest, how good a job would you say *I* do?'

Under the shaded lighting of the room, I couldn't make out whether she was surveying me seriously or with a quirk of the lips. 'The best, I imagine, within the limits of your brief.'

'Is that a compliment?'

'Take it how you like. Most of us are prisoners of our environment, let's face it.'

'You mean, we're hemmed in by outside forces that none of us really comprehend? Balancing what's practical with what our consciences can stand?'

'Sounds feasible,' she said, with a hiccup. 'If I knew what it meant.'

'Sorry. This is all getting a bit pseudo. On a lighter note—'

'There's a lot of nastiness around,' she said suddenly, 'wherever you look. Question is, should one ignore it, record it, or try like crazy to do something about it?'

'The last two, maybe. In tandem.'

A soundless sigh ran visibly through her. 'More wine? No? You'll have to help me finish the bottle . . . I'm getting morbid. It's what you said in the car, about Lionel. I was just thinking, if he were to walk through that door now, this minute . . . I'm not sure what I'd do. He was such a pain. He wrecked my life: mine and Gerald's. And yet, outside these four walls, everyone idolized him as God's gift to the Entertainment of the People. Which I suppose he was, after a fashion.'

I looked at her inquiringly. 'What exactly did he do?'

'Head of Programming for PST.' She said it dispassionately, as though referring to a once-dreaded malignant disease that she had come to terms with. 'He was responsible for all the garbage that went out at peak hours, five days a week, on Channel Fourteen.'

'I never knew that.'

'You do now.' She refilled her glass. 'It's my guilty secret. I only talk about it when I'm sloshed.'

'Why should you feel guilt?'

'Because in the early days, heaven help me, I encouraged him. Slaved like a maniac to foster his damn career. I've a lot to answer for.'

There seemed nothing to say. Having half-emptied her glass again, she heaved another sigh, audibly this time, and kicked off her slippers, leaving them to lie on the carpet. 'After the bust-up,' she said reminiscently, 'he did the first decent thing in his life and emigrated, to my unuttera—to my huge relief.'

'Where to?'

'Down Under. He's now programming them all in Sydney, for their sins. How far is that? Twelve thousand miles? Doesn't seem a lot, when you say it fast. That's enough about Lionel. How's Elaine making out with her rehearsals?'

I explained that I had seen little of her for several days. 'We're not really talking. I said something about the theatre which annoyed her, so Daddy's in the doghouse. But she seems to be working pretty hard.'

Laura sat up a little. 'Fighting with both girls at once? Hardly your style, Peter.'

'Both quarrels,' I said ruefully, 'stemmed from the same root.' With a fingernail I pinged the rim of my wineglass. 'She'll come round. Next Monday, with any luck.'

'Why Monday?'

'We're running a pre-first night splash on the production. Story and pictures.'

Laura contemplated me in silence before draining her glass. 'Yup,' she said, planking it down and inspecting the bottle. 'That ought to do something.'

I wasn't sure what she meant, but I let it pass. 'Incidentally,' I said, 'Andy Kent will be coming with us to the opening night. You don't mind?'

'Why should I mind? I told you, we're old mates.' Splashing the last of the wine into her glass, she tossed the empty bottle into a nest of cushions on a nearby sofa and sat back again to brood at the ceiling. 'If it were anyone of a dozen others I could mention . . . Sorry, Peter. I'm only a man-hater in my cups. Not even then, to be honest. But I generally find it expedient to pretend to be. Saves a lot of embarrassment.' She hiccuped. 'To me and to others.'

I observed her doubtfully. 'Where do I stand in all this?'

'For the moment, you're helping me to get plastered. There's another bottle outside.'

I fetched the other bottle. Replenishing the two glasses, I said tentatively, 'If it's not specifically me, and it's not pressure of toil, it must be the retrospect analysis. Bad for the soul.'

'You're quite perceptive at times, you know that?' Once more she sat up to stare at the brimming glass between her fingers. Presently she said, 'When do you plan to write your novel?'

'I don't plan to.'

'One novelist in the family's enough, huh? Praise the Lord.'

'I doubt if that's the reason. I just don't think I'd be very good. What I'm doing suits me well enough . . . that is, I thought it did.'

'Until the mental quibbles started creeping in?' Laura's gaze became abstracted. Finally she went on, 'You've quite a bit going for you. Journalistic flair. A nose for the topical. Leadership qualities. In your own slightly offbeat way, you inspire people. That counts for a lot.'

I said lightly, 'And you'd rank yourself as one of the inspired?'

She remained silent. From the table where I had opened the bottle, I went across and lowered myself on to the arm of her chair, keeping a few careful inches of space between us. 'There's something,' I told her, examining my shoes, 'I'd like you to know. I don't think I'd have been enjoying the job so much, or inspiring people so effectively, if you hadn't been around. Does that surprise you?'

'Not greatly,' she said with candour.

'You've been half-expecting me to blurt out something of the kind?'

'Half-hoping.'

We looked at one another. The dark circles around her eyes, more pronounced than usual, gave her an appearance at once world-weary and expectant. I said, 'This dialogue's suffering from galloping inflation. It could do with the blue pencil.'

'You're the editor.'

During the kiss she kept herself very still. When I drew back, she continued looking across the room for a moment or two before saying, a little shakily, 'I think you managed to sub me right out. I'm speechless.'

'We can always write in a phrase or two later,' I told her. 'For the moment, you don't mind if we substitute action for words?'

CHAPTER 15

Elaine hadn't gone to bed. Swathed in a dressing-gown, she was huddled on the studio couch in the living-room, nibbling a dry biscuit, watching a late horror movie on television. From the doorway I inquired brightly, 'Wakeful tonight?'

'Didn't feel like sleeping.' Deserting the couch, she flicked the action dismissively from the screen and turned away to the sideboard. 'Want a drink?'

'What are we celebrating?'

'Do you want one?' There was a faint stress on the third word. For a moment I regarded her silently.

'At this rate, I'm evidently going to need one.'

Wordlessly she poured a Scotch, adding soda in a brief squirt that sounded like an expletive. For herself, she half-filled a glass with lemon juice and topped it with vodka. Dumping both glasses on the coffee-table, she re-established herself on the extreme edge of the couch at one end to sit in a hunch, staring down at the polished table-surface as if using it to determine whether or not her make-up had been thoroughly removed. Hauling a footstool to the other side of the table, I lowered myself on to it and lifted the Scotch.

'Mine, I take it?'

She said, 'What's this I've been hearing from Jimmy?'

'I don't know, Elaine. What have you heard?'

'This myth about a double-page spread in the *Planet*. Whose inspiration was that? As if one need ask.'

I waited a moment, letting the first gulp of whisky swish around and impede anything too hasty. Presently I replied reasonably, 'You're referring, I assume, to our plan for some illustrated coverage of the latest Backstage production in rehearsal. As a cast member, you don't seem wild about the idea.'

Her shoulders moved convulsively inside the dressing-gown, a green-and-vermilion fluffball that gave her the appearance of a Dresden doll wrapped in a tea-cosy. A doll with teeth. 'Do me a big favour, will you? Try not to behave like a patronizing parent. It doesn't suit you.'

I breathed with depth and regularity for five seconds. 'It was a board decision, in fact.'

'Dad. Don't insult my intelligence.'

'The idea didn't come from me.'

'Of course not.'

'I had nothing to do with it. Our acting Governor summoned me and issued his orders. I had no choice.'

She looked directly at me for the first time. 'You expect me to believe that?'

'What you believe, Elaine,' I said formally, 'is for you to decide. I'd just be grateful if you'd be so kind as to give me some credit for being worthy of special consideration. Offhand, I can't recall ever having lied to you. If you know otherwise, perhaps you'll refresh my memory.'

'You sound like one of your own editorials.' The sulkiness in her voice was shadowed by a wisp of humour, immediately submerged by an eruption of righteous anger. 'I'm not talking about past occasions. It's this one that concerns me. It's so *cheap*. What are you trying to do—curry your way back into favour with a blank cheque? What did you expect *me* to do? Fall on your neck with sobs of gratitude? Thanks a million, Dad. We're so charmed with the free publicity, Dad. I'll never be horrid again, I'll depend on you for—'

'Stop it, Elaine.'

My own wrath imparted a pistol-crack to the command, bringing her down in flight. She glared blindly across the room, breathing fast. Between sips of unwanted Scotch I did much the same. Slowly the atmosphere cooled to boiling-point. I set my glass down with a thump.

'Whatever you may think—and I suppose I can't altogether blame you for thinking it—the fact is that Alan Turnbull called me to his lair, asked about the production, saw its possibilities, suggested a spread, instructed me not to duck it just because I was your father. Like it or not, I do work under guidelines. I'm in no position to ignore directives.'

Elaine said nothing.

'Besides which,' I added, 'if you want to know, I happen to consider it's a sound idea in its own right. Rick Smythe is news. If your Jimmy isn't now, he soon will be. As for you . . . Objective judgement tells me you're the stage bombshell of the near future, regardless of whether your surname is Rodgers or . . . Blenkinsop. So would you oblige me by not flying off the handle?'

When she spoke again, it was on a calmer key. 'Leaving aside the pros and cons, I still don't like it. Everyone will assume it was a fix. I don't *want* it to be like that. I want to arrive under my own steam. I want—'

'You'll get there on your own. No question. And since you're firmly on your way to stardom, why shouldn't the *Planet* be first to call attention to the fact? He's no philan-thropist, our Alan Turnbull. If it's pictures of you he wants, it's because he thinks you'll help sell copies. It's not us doing you a favour. It's the other way round.'

Elaine sat staring at me. Feeling a sudden intense weariness, I ran fingers through my hair and leaned back.

Too late, I remembered that I was on a footstool, not a chair. The deep pile of the carpet tempered the impact, but my spine still felt as if it had been backed up with some violence against a concrete post. My legs flew humiliatingly above the level of the rest of me, wavered in mid-air for a moment, then collapsed back to the floor. The footstool, which was on castors, shot away to my right.

From her place on the couch, Elaine gaped down at me. An assortment of expressions seemed to be struggling for supremacy over her face, which was acquiring a depth of colour to match the crimson covers on the furniture. Her lower lip began to wobble.

Clambering up with the aid of the coffee-table, I did some exploratory work on the lumbar region with my fingertips before stumping away to retrieve the stool. As I wheeled it back, Elaine's features broke up. A squeal of pure delight broke from her. Flinging herself back against cushions, she surrendered to torrents of mirth.

Replacing myself on the stool, I said grumpily, 'I might have done myself a mischief.'

The remark sent her off again. Between paroxysms she fought to utter. 'Dad—you're priceless. Is this how you . . . board meetings . . . I can just . . .'

'I'm not on the board.'

'You certainly were then.' Elaine exploded again all over the couch. Capitulating, I joined her. For the next minute and a half we rolled about, free of inhibition, regardless of the sensitivities of other block-dwellers above and below us at one o'clock in the morning. By the time recovery set in, the armistice document had been signed, sealed and stored away. The closing embrace was a formality, but none the less pleasant for all that, and an almighty relief: a near-intolerable weight had been lifted from me. The balance-sheet of the evening showed a sizeable credit.

To mark the patch-up, Elaine made coffee. 'Having got this far, we may as well make a night of it,' she remarked, laying out cups in her old style and plying me with biscuits. 'I can't face going to bed yet. I'm still fired up from rehearsal.'

'Went with a bang, did it?'

'Not the kind you mean. Jimmy was on edge. He bawled each of us out at least twice.'

'What had made him twitchy?'

Elaine scratched her head, dislodging a coppery tress at which she gazed vacantly before replacing it behind an ear. 'I think he gets worried about that disabled brother of his. Then there's all the hassle with his rivals.'

'Rivals?'

'Showbiz competitors,' she enlarged vaguely. 'Jimmy's always had this thing about the canned product. Thinks the screen exponents get too much support at the expense of live theatre.'

'Who from?'

'Backers, sponsors, the Government. People in general. The media.'

'That's a bit steep,' I protested. 'Who's giving him a centre-spread next Monday?'

'Oh, he's grateful for that. More so than I was,' she added slyly, 'up to ten minutes ago. But this is the whole point. The reason he welcomes anything of the kind is that it's so rare. Normally, we have to flog on in isolation while films and television get all the attention . . . and the handouts. It does grate a bit, at times.'

'*C'est la vie.* Surely his art sustains him?'

'Of course it does. He wouldn't stick with it, otherwise. It doesn't alter the fact that he gets irked when he runs up against production problems and can't get help to overcome them. Then he takes it out on us.'

'Tough on the cast.'

'We know he doesn't mean it. It's just an outlet. He was sweeter than honey again when he brought me home tonight. Which reminds me, Dad . . .' Elaine fixed me with a survey half-indulgent, half-accusatory. 'You were looking fairly pleased with yourself when you came in just now, before I said my little piece. What put you in such a good mood?'

'We outsold the *Record* again last month,' I said complacently.

'Is that all?'

'Not quite,' I admitted. 'I've just enjoyed a rather good evening with Laura.'

'Laura Cadey, the Woman's Editor?' Elaine's inspection gained overtones of a kind of fond severity. 'Get on well with her, do you?'

I looked straight back at her. 'Does that bother you?'

Leaning across, she put a hand on my wrist and squeezed it. 'Why ever should it? Good luck, Dad. You deserve it.'

'Not sure that I do,' I said, with sudden gloom. 'There's Katie, still. Distant as ever. I wish I could talk to her.'

Elaine gave me another squeeze. 'She'll gravitate back when she's ready. But not in response to open invitations in the Press, you daft journalist. Of all the half-baked schemes. I could have told you she'd never fall for that one.'

CHAPTER 16

'Before we go,' I said to Andy, 'have you got the street layout nicely imprinted on your brain?'

'I think so.'

'Find yourself a weapon?'

A little sheepishly he unzipped his jacket to expose, strapped to his chest, what looked like the leg of a sideboard. 'If we hit trouble,' he muttered, 'I'll probably spend three minutes trying to unhitch the thing, but it was the best I could do. Got something figured out?'

I stared at the street plan. 'Several possibilities spring to mind. I still think the alleyway scheme is the most promising. It's just a few yards along from the Platter, practically pitch-dark, and invariably has mountains of garbage in plastic sacks piled along it every night. I can vouch for that: I've checked. Also, the back end of it comes out into a square which is hardly noticeable for animation by day, never mind any other time.' I glanced at him with a sick grin. 'Ideal mugging territory, wouldn't you say?'

'Too right. If you're thinking of putting it to the test, you must be—'

'Only under controlled conditions, as the lab boys say. I'm relying on you, Andy.'

'That's what paralyses me.'

'How's this for a schedule? At nine-thirty, say, on the button, I emerge from the restaurant. In a clear voice, I inform the doorman that I intend to take a stroll . . .'

'Like John Wallington?'

'Exactly like him. Having conveyed the message to all and sundry, I then make brazenly for the mouth of the alley-way, turn into it as though taking a short cut towards Knightsbridge—which it is—and keep walking, slowly and pensively, like a man with something on his mind . . . Do I sound an inviting target?'

'You sound like a strolling disaster. What's controlled about all that?'

'For one thing, I'll be on my guard.'

'How's your unarmed combat, these days?'

'For another, you'll be keeping a close eye on me.'

'Silly question, I know, but where from?'

'About here.' I stabbed with a thumb. 'That's where the rubbish sacks are usually piled highest. It's a stretch of blank wall: no windows or doorways. You could hide there indefinitely, no problem.'

Andy looked less than captivated by the prospect. 'What if someone hikes along and dumps more bags on me while I'm waiting?'

'Extra cover,' I said unkindly. 'Don't worry, they're all sealed and pollution-free. Totally hygienic.'

'You're not going to be the one using them as cushions.'

'Would you rather we swapped roles?'

'I'd rather we ditched the whole plan.' He gazed down at the street map. 'There's something else you may not have considered.'

'What's that?'

'Let's assume the publicity has had its effect and there's an assassin out there, waiting to have a tilt at you. What's to stop him adopting a similar procedure? What if he decides to hide among the garbage sacks, prior to—'

'Then you can tell each other filthy stories to pass the time.' I shook my head with an assurance I was far from feeling. 'Anyone with plans for me would hardly wait in a dark alley, would they? I might not walk that way. They'd need to have a continual view of the restaurant, so as to be able to follow me when I came out.'

'Anyone hanging around the street would stick out like a false nose.'

'What's the matter with the place itself? The cocktail bar has a first-class view of the main entrance and foyer.'

He blinked. 'That's true.'

'Anyone could drink quietly there for an entire evening without drawing much attention.'

'Holding a blunt instrument?'

'Briefcase,' I suggested. 'Instrument case.' I paused. 'Typewriter case. It only wants a touch of imagination.'

'Hmph,' said Andy. 'For both our sakes, let's hope yours is running away with you.'

★

Two or three Press photographers, known to me by sight, were already on station by the striped awning that protected the footway between kerb and entrance. I greeted them breezily. 'Hi, boys. Come to record the reunion?'

They produced apologetic simpers. The doorman hissed into my ear. 'If they're going to be a nuisance, Mr Rodgers, you can leave by the back way. Or you and your daughter could—'

'It's all right, Ferdy. I doubt if Katie's going to show up. If they want a shot of my hangdog expression as I'm leaving, they're welcome.' I gave him a straight look. 'Who knows? It might tip the scales, bring her running back.' To the photographers I said affably, 'Stick around, you blokes. I'm not planning to take long over the meal.'

My remarks were pitched on a key calculated to waft them through the entrance lobby to the cocktail bar, which comprised an open-ended alcove to the right. Strolling past, I took swift note of its occupancy. Three or four men and an elderly woman were on stools at the bar counter: a dozen more were dispersed among the tables. I recognized nobody.

The restaurant itself was busier. Claiming my reserved table for two by the furthermost wall, I ordered a martini and sat back in a relaxed manner to wait, sheltered by a copy of the evening paper that I had taken care to bring along. As a refuge, newsprint may be old hat but it remains unbeatable. From behind cover, I was able to pass a discreet eye over the remainder of the tables, some of whose inhabitants were wearisomely familiar. The standard mix. Politicians, City people, showbiz names. Jeremy Hickster of the *Record* was there, commanding his favourite table for six at the far side. We exchanged semi-abusive waves. After that, I noticed him talking animatedly to his five guests, three of whom were women: all of them were sending covert glances my way. I feigned not to see.

Company would have helped. I wished it could have been

Laura. Before leaving Planet House I had tried to get in touch with her, but she had been out of the building. She was dining, Meg Saunders had reported, with a visiting female playwright from New York and would not be back in the office until ten at the earliest. My sense of let-down had been acute and unreasonable. Despite what had occurred, I had no special claim upon Laura . . . yet. I should merely have liked the chance of a bracing word. Possibly, however, it would have proved counter-productive, weakened my resolve. Thrusting thoughts of her aside, I ordered a crab salad.

No sign of Katie. I hadn't really been expecting it, but her non-appearance still added to my depression, although it simplified the task I had set myself. A task which, from within the warmth and hubbub of The Gourmet Platter, tended to acquire an increasingly ludicrous quality. Was it worth going through with? I had coffee while thinking about it. My watch told me it was nine-twenty. Right on schedule. With a mental shrug I called for the bill.

Hawk-eyed as ever, Jeremy Hickster signalled to me. Resignedly I went across. Contrary to my expectation, he didn't crow. There was very nearly a note of sympathy in his voice. 'No Cordelia, then? So much for the power of the Press. Sorry about that, old son.'

I had a few phrases on hand, pre-moulded for the eventuality. 'Can't say I blame Katie for not taking me up. It was just an idea—maybe not a very good one.'

A female member of the party said compassionately, 'Will you be trying again, Mr Rodgers?'

'I doubt it. If my daughter feels like making contact, in her own time, I'll be available.'

Hickster made a hospitable gesture. 'Join us? Better than finishing the evening on a downbeat.'

'Thanks, but I need some exercise.' With an all-embracing nod I returned to my table, settled the bill, collected my coat

and walked out to the lobby. The occupancy of the cocktail
bar seemed to have changed somewhat, but I gave it only the
sketchiest of inspections. I had almost ceased to care. Outside, the original group of photographers around the awning
had been swollen by others: there were seven in all. Somehow, this planted the seal of idiocy upon the evening. Bracing
myself, I arranged my features and presented myself at the
entrance.

'Such activity,' I remarked genially, as cameras flashed.

'What now, Mr Rodgers? Any other plans for a reconcili-
ation?'

'That's up to my daughter. It's for her to decide, and I
shall respect her wishes.'

'Any regrets about approaching it in this way?'

'The only thing I regret is the misunderstanding that led
up to it.' I glanced at my watch. 'Anything else? I'm rather
anxious for a quiet walk before getting back into harness. I'm
sure you understand.'

Tactfully they stood aside. Descending the steps to the
pavement, I turned left and set off at a modest pace, hunch-
shouldered as if lost in thought. The night air was sharp but
dry. There was the faintest of breezes. For a constitutional,
conditions were perfect: nothing could have been more
natural than for a dejected parent to walk off by himself,
nursing bruised feelings.

Nor to pause at the mouth of the alleyway and glance
around as if checking for traffic. The movement showed me a
deserted street. The photographers had dispersed. The
Platter's main entrance had reverted to tranquillity. In
the manner of one who, on a whim, had revised his plans, I
took another look at my watch and turned into the gloom
of the alley.

The darkness was, in fact, less blanketing than I had
envisaged. Two or three low-power bulbs attached to the
walls put out enough light to run spectral fingers over the

bulging plastic sacks heaped erratically against the brick-work, striking from them a pale gleam like that of polished coal in a cellar. Pacing slowly, head down, I went past them in apparent oblivion to the halfway point. Here, abreast of an exterior metal staircase that went upwards to nowhere, I halted to take out a handkerchief, blow my nose.

The largest rubbish pile now lay behind me, to my right. Skirting it, I had cleared my throat twice, as prearranged. The lack of response had been disconcerting. Which was illogical, since I myself had insisted upon this exact pro-cedure. An unreasonable annoyance with Andy took hold of me. He could have bent the rules. Stuffing the handkerchief away, I resumed my snail-pace progress, listening to the sound-effects. Shoe-leather on concrete. Evocative stuff. The kind of thing dear to the hearts of movie directors. Sight, when you thought about it, was not so important. Ears were what counted. Why did the blind get all the pity? Without the ability to hear . . .

It wasn't a sound that froze me. More of a sensation: a pulse of air at the nape. As though a palm-leaf had lazily been flapped, three inches to the rear. Alleys, I had time to think, attracted wind-currents. For all that, it seemed only prudent to turn. I had started to do so when, from immediately to my left, the wall fell on me.

The gnawing ache at the base of my neck seemed to demand a change of position, so I groped for the pillows. It was puzzling not to find them. It might have been irritating, except that irritation was beyond my immediate resources.

The puzzlement lingered. All that had met my fingertips was a hard, rippled surface, frigid, like a frozen pond. What had become of the bed-sheets?

A voice boomed in my left ear. 'Lie still. Don't try to move.'

If Elaine was practising a spot of lesbian vocal delivery,

she was making a spectacular job of it. I wished she would find the pillows. Turning on to my side, I met the same unyielding reception and heard a moan. The voice drummed again. 'Take it easy. You may be concussed.'

Lying still obediently, trying to work out why somebody should be saying that, I discovered that I felt chilled through. Action on this front seemed imperative. I sat up.

The wall hit me again. Less comprehensively this time, but it still packed plenty of clout. Something shot up from my throat and emerged as a groan. When the echoes had begun to die away, I made my eyes focus. The thing they focused upon was a set of features which, in stages, assembled themselves into the face of Andy: from close range, he was watching me intently. Seeing recognition dawn, he puffed his cheeks.

'I was afraid you might have . . .'

He left the phrase incomplete, or had my ears closed up? 'Might've what?' I mumbled. I groped for the seat of the fire inside my neck. 'D'you have anything for rheumatism?'

'For Christ's sake.' He sounded angry. 'What you need is an X-ray.'

Struggling to make sense of the assertion, I noticed that the brick walls of the alley were still upright. So they hadn't collapsed on me. Memory began to dribble back.

'It worked, then?'

'If you want to put it that way.' Supporting me with an arm, Andy was manifestly a victim of contrition and fury in measured proportions. 'Didn't I say we should leave it to the cops? They know what they're up to.'

'Who was it?' An obscure excitement was creeping up on my dizziness. 'Did you get a look?'

'He took off.' Andy pointed towards the square beyond the alley. 'I lost him. Couldn't leave you here—I had to come back. I should have prevented him hitting you in the first place.'

'Never mind that. Where did he come from?'

'How the hell would I know?' Andy was feeling for my pulse, amateurishly but with dedication. 'It all happened so fast. One second you were passing me: the next, there was this figure swooping from somewhere . . .'

'Holding anything?'

'Something square, I think, like a parcel. You need attention. Wait while I call a—'

'No, Andy, forget it. I'm all right. Just help me to stand up . . .'

A few moments later I said shakily, 'Okay, so I need another minute on this dustbin. You didn't by any chance snatch a glimpse of his face?'

'It happened so *fast*.' Andy's gaze roamed upwards, probing the metal stairway. 'Wait a second . . .'

His boots clashed on the steel rungs. On his return, he brandished a despairing arm. 'Door at the top, but it's locked. If someone was waiting half way up, how did I miss spotting him? Doesn't make sense. If somebody—'

'There's another thing that makes no sense, Andy. That's blaming yourself. I did ask for it.'

'Where's the nearest nick?'

'Forget about the cops. It's pointless.'

'They should at least know,' he objected.

'Why? What can they do?'

He looked nonplussed. I added, 'We're a step further on. We now know that the letter was no idle threat . . . unless tonight's incident was pure coincidence, which I think we can discount. Help me up.'

This time I succeeded in staying on my feet while the alley came gradually to a halt around me. After a few moments I felt stable enough to be steered by Andy to the other side of the square, where the Cavalier was parked. Toppling into the passenger seat, I sat passive while he went wordlessly to the driver's side and did efficient things to ignition and gears.

'I'll take you straight home,' he announced. 'You need—'

'No. Back to E.C.4., thanks. I left some things at the office.'

'Forget them for tonight. You're in no state—'

'Don't argue,' I implored, and rested my head.

The motion of the vehicle reactivated the giddiness inside my skull. Bracing myself against the cornering, I kept my eyes open because shutting them made it worse. Thoughts pounded through my brain, adding to the discomfort. With hindsight, I was starting to realize that I had miscalculated badly: I had thought I was being circumspect, but in the event the pair of us had been out-manœuvred with disheartening ease. I was out of my league. In the space of a few reckless seconds, Katie and Elaine might well have found themselves orphans, and the editor's chair at the *Planet* could have become vacant. It was the kind of reflection that didn't mix well with cranial vertigo.

As we reached the crest of Piccadilly, Andy said morosely, 'I never appreciated it could happen so *fast*. If I'd only—'

'Will you stop saying that? But for you, I could have been on a slab by now. Tell me something,' I went on hastily, to take his mind off it. 'Remember that typewriter you mentioned?'

'The Laski? I've made inquiries,' he assured me, crossing the lights at amber. 'The dealer I flogged it to told me an agency took it. He was—'

'What sort of an agency?'

'Secretarial employment. I went round there. They told me it had been bought from them by one of their temps who wanted a machine of her own to take about with her. Yes, I chased her up as well. She still has it.'

I caressed the back of my neck. 'What kind of a woman . . . ?'

'Just a youngster. Eighteen or thereabouts.'

'Heavy build?'

'Thin as a lath. Comes up to my shoulder. We can forget her.'

'It was just an idea,' I said despondently. 'You didn't think to ask, I suppose, about the places she's worked at recently?'

'She's only had one switch. At the moment she's with a merchant bank in Fenchurch Street, has been for the past week. Before that she spent three and a half months with a West End firm of theatrical costumiers. All fairly innocuous.'

I sighed. 'The Laski's a tenuous link, anyway. Rare it may be, but yours can't be the only one still around.' I paused. 'Theatrical costumiers? Who do they supply?'

Andy steered deftly out of Haymarket. 'Drama world in general, presumably. I stopped digging at that point. Something in your mind?'

My headshake proved too painful to prolong. 'I'm clutching at straws. Theatre . . . entertainment world . . . current holocaust . . . Am I giving way to delirium?'

'I don't know,' he said, shooting me an appraising look. 'Still want me to take you to Planet House?'

'Keep going. There's safety in numbers.'

Andy snorted, but held his peace.

CHAPTER 17

Laura was back at her desk, gazing pensively at the screen of her word-processor. At sight of me she ignited a smile, then doused it.

'Peter, you look ghastly. What's the trouble?'

I subsided on to a leather-topped bench against the wall. 'For one thing, Katie didn't show.'

'I'm sorry. But you weren't really expecting it, were you?' She examined me more closely. 'Or were you?'

'I dare say one always hopes. It wasn't just that, though. I was mugged.'

'Oh no!' She sprang up and came across. 'Badly?'

'Just a cosh behind the ear. Nothing taken. Andy saw to that.'

'Andy? He was with you?'

I related the evening's events, plus the scheming behind them. Having listened expressionlessly, Laura delivered her opinion: it was concise and pungent. I assented humbly to all she said. Disarmed by my lack of fight, she joined me on the bench, placed an arm across my shoulders and added, 'It was a damn fool venture, Peter, but I suppose you wouldn't be who you are if you didn't go out on a limb occasionally. Just don't try it too often. Like an aspirin?'

'I thought you'd never ask.'

'Headache bad?'

'Is there a good variety?'

'Check-up for you, my lad,' she declared. 'I'll drive you round to the—'

'No, Laura. Thanks all the same. That wasn't the reason I came back here.'

'I can't think why you did. Andy should have run you straight home.'

'I didn't want to alarm Elaine. She'd only fuss. That's bad for her work concentration, and besides . . .'

'Don't tell me. She'd also have a go at you, and you know perfectly well you deserve it. You're scared of her,' Laura said severely, quitting the bench to walk over to her desk and slide open a drawer.

'We've only just got back on matey terms,' I said defensively. 'I'd hate to wreck things again. She's been lecturing me for weeks. Something like this might be all she needs to have me committed or something.'

'You could well be right.' Removing a small carton from the drawer, Laura scowled at it. 'I don't have aspirin, but these are good. They've got paracetamol in them—better for the stomach. I'll fetch you a coffee to take them with.'

She returned presently from the corridor vending machine with a brimming beaker. Despite my condition, I was appreciatively aware once more of the way she moved, the style of her appearance. The dark, close-fitting trouser suit she was wearing matched exactly her personality: it was good-looking, it was sensible, it detracted in no way from her essential femaleness, the allure that clung to her like a web of subtle tint. Accepting the beaker, I bowled down the two tablets she handed me, spluttered a little, took a couple more sips of the inky fluid and gave it back to her. 'Remind me to speak to the board about having humans installed. They couldn't come up with a worse brew. How did you make out with the Yankee play-scribbler?'

'Something of a squandered evening, I fear.'

'Don't tell me she didn't talk.'

'Oh, she talked. She never did another thing from start to finish, but as for *saying* anything . . . If I get a line out of it, I'll be amazed.'

'Pity,' I said, trying to develop a professional interest. 'What's her name?'

'Moira Bechstein. Very small, very intense . . . very Bronx. That says it all. You don't want to hear about her,' Laura concluded, studying me closely with folded arms. 'First things first. Have you talked to the police yet?'

'They're not coming into this.'

'But they must!'

At some personal cost, I shook my head again. 'I don't want them involved. The whole thing could leak out.'

'So? If it did, it might have the effect of warning the culprit off.'

'He hasn't seemed easily discouraged, up to now. The thing I want to avoid is a lot of well-meaning advice from people who can't see beyond their noses. It's—'

Laura snorted. 'If you ask me, you could use some.'

'Yes, but Laura, don't you see? I'm still the best hope of bringing him into the open. He's had a bash at me and he's failed . . . he's not going to like that, if I'm any judge.'

The stare she gave me was more eloquent than her words. 'You mean, you intend to keep yourself deliberately in the firing-line? Keep sticking your neck out?'

I winced. 'I'd sooner it was some other place. But broadly, yes, that about summarizes the position. Using the utmost caution—'

'You're mad, Peter. Off your rocker.'

'I thrive on encouragement. All I know is,' I said stubbornly, 'if I give up now and just hand it to the police to investigate, I'll have it on my conscience that I might be demolishing the best chance there is of preventing future violence. If I can only . . .'

I lost the thread. Pain was lancing my head. Closing my eyes, I kept them shut for what seemed like an hour: when I reopened them she was still standing there, watching me with a kind of exasperated fondness. I essayed a grin of reassurance. 'Feel like running me home now? I'm nearly dropping off.'

She was a better driver than Andy, or else I was further gone. All the way to the apartment, I was only dimly and spasmodically conscious of movement; most of the time, in full recline on the Strada's front passenger seat, I dozed and dreamt dizzily while the street lamps pierced the shadow overhead.

'Want some breakfast?'

The voice reached me from the distant end of a brick tunnel. Crawling through it, I came gradually in sight of Elaine. Her face, at least. It was above mine, looking down with an appearance of anxiety. Opening my mouth to say something, I forgot what my brain had formulated. Elaine continued instead. 'Don't try to sit up. You look as if—'

'Wait a bit.'

Turning on to my stomach, I half-throttled a groan as fire darted through my skull. Presently, with a thrust of both arms, I hoisted myself to a crouch and stayed there until the bed had stopped bucking. Slowly I pivoted back into a leaning posture, braced by my elbows. Through surges of head-pain I got her more or less into focus. 'Why shouldn't I sit up?'

Elaine betrayed impatience. 'Don't try to pretend. You were barely half-conscious when Laura staggered in with you last night.'

'I asked her not to—'

'We arrived back together. What was she meant to do, hand you over without a word?'

I blinked several times, futilely. 'What did she tell you?'

'Said you'd met with some mishap in your office. Hit your head on a lamp bracket, or something. It took the two of us about twenty minutes to heave you into bed.' Stabilizing the tray she was holding against the pillows, Elaine sat on the rim of the mattress to examine me sternly. 'You're sure it wasn't a whisky bottle?'

'What?'

'The thing you bashed yourself against.'

'Nothing like that, my dear, I promise. I was a bit impetuous leaping out of my office chair, that's all. My head collided with an attachment on the back. I've done it before, only less drastically.'

'Try to control yourself. Were you stunned?'

'I believe I was out for a while.' Reversion to the truth, if only momentarily, came as a relief.

Elaine clicked her tongue. 'And you say I flap too much. You can't even look after yourself when you're sitting at your own desk. No wonder Laura was concerned. She's just phoned. I said I'd find out how you were feeling, and call her back. And while I'm at it,' Elaine added, abandoning the mattress, 'I'll summon the quack. Lie still and swig some coffee. It's fresh.'

'Come back here, Elaine. I don't need a doctor.'

'You don't need concussion. Or a hairline fracture.'

'Will you stop dramatizing? I'm quite okay. Or shall be, when I've re-caffeinated myself. You're not to dream of bringing a doctor in here.'

'Right,' she said, ambiguously.

Her expression as she left the room was one that I recognized. I had seen it a hundred times on the face of her mother. Resignedly pouring coffee—a drinkable version, in contrast to the previous evening's poison—I directed it at the seat of the blaze that was continuing to send tongues of flame on scouting missions into the back of my neck. It did nothing to extinguish them, but the nausea that resulted was at least a distraction. Lying back, breathing with desperate regularity in a bid to combat the sensation, I awaited the arrival of someone from our local group practice. Knowing Elaine, I estimated the delay at no more than an hour.

Meanwhile I reviewed the situation.

In the pale light of dawn, my bravado of a few hours previously had largely evaporated. Could Laura be right? Was it time to call a halt? Criminal investigation, I was fond of declaiming from editorial heights, was something best left to those qualified and equipped for the role: had the stage been reached where I should pursue my own advice? Common sense suggested that it had. Laura must be right.

Telling myself that my decision was made, I swallowed a morsel or two of dry toast, sipped more coffee, again felt a little sick, then drowsy, and drifted back into semi-oblivion.

I was wrong about the doctor. It was three hours before he turned up. By then I had slept deeply: on awakening I felt inert, but the sharp edge of the cranial discomfort had been blunted. It was now eleven-fifteen. The GP, a young Anglo-

Indian, examined me impassively, shone a torch into my eyes, asked me three times what day of the week it was, and pronounced finally that I must go to a casualty outpatients department for an X-ray. When I protested, he merely scrawled a few lines on a sheet of paper and handed it to Elaine with instructions that I was to be got there by one-thirty.

'But I'm feeling much better,' I said, with partial accuracy. 'Why waste their time?'

'They've some to spare,' he replied briefly, and went.

In a sense, he was right. They seemed to have plenty available, and they took it. Our return to the apartment in the Cavalier, which Elaine had journeyed by taxi to Planet House to retrieve from the basement, was not achieved until after four o'clock. On the credit side, I had been cleared for breakages, while being admonished to take things quietly for a day or two and get plenty of rest. I rang through again to Wally Farr, with whom I had spoken earlier. He urged me to stay home at least until Monday.

'Everything's cruising along,' he said comfortably. 'No panics. Why not stay in an armchair with your feet up? Just watch how you climb out of it, that's all.'

My established fable, which I had repeated both to him and to the radiographer, seemed to have carried enough weight to convince. Neither of them had voiced incredulity at such an occurrence, although each had chortled. I said, 'Don't worry, I've no desire for a second performance. I'll leave things to you then, Wally, for the weekend. Enjoy yourself.'

Five seconds after downing the receiver, I had a call from Andy. 'Been trying to get you for hours,' he said, sounding harassed. 'Any comebacks after last night?'

I explained about the X-rays and the all-clear. 'Thanks for keeping quiet about the cause. Saved a lot of complications.'

'Don't mention it,' he said drily. 'Seen the papers?'

'One or two.' I had read them while awaiting the X-ray. 'Did me proud, didn't they? Doting dad jilted by doubting daughter. I suppose I asked for it. Listen, Andy, I'm thinking matters over. I may decide to go to the police, after all, but stay quiet about it in the meantime, will you? We'll talk about it again on Monday.'

'You're probably doing the right thing. Watch yourself.'

In a couple of the rival Fleet Street tabloids, I had been shown emerging disconsolately from the Gourmet under such jokey headlines as No KATIE FOR PETER and DAD'S VIGIL IN VAIN. Below, I was quoted imaginatively as saying things like, 'She didn't show up, but I enjoyed the soup,' and, on a more lugubrious note, 'To get things sorted out with her, I'll come back here as often as it takes.' Others, among them Jeremy Hickster, had relied solely on text of a highly fictional nature, most of it just skirting the rim of libel. Having anticipated no better, I was able to take it all in my stride. Elaine was less tolerant.

'They've made you look a complete idiot, Dad. You must have known what you were letting yourself in for. Katie won't be overjoyed, either.'

'I'll explain things to her, in due course.'

'Assuming you get the chance. At this rate she'll stay out of your way indefinitely, and I can't say I'd blame her.'

Relenting over tea and scones, Elaine then informed me that she had secured, through Jimmy, three complimentary tickets for the first night at The Backstage, and had sent a fourth to Katie. 'If it reaches her and she decides to come, your paths might cross. Don't count on it, though. Katie might see through the dodge. She's quite sharp when she's upset.'

'I'd noticed. Thanks anyway, love, for the effort.' I glanced up from spreading honey. 'Isn't it tonight we're looking in on you at rehearsal?'

Elaine grimaced. 'Friday night is *Planet* night. We all have to be ready with the quotable quotes, right?'

'Treat the lads kindly.' Biting into the scone, I chewed meditatively while watching her add hot water to the teapot. At times like this, it was difficult to visualize Elaine on stage, clad frequently in very little, striking poses and talking in regional accents. In home surroundings she was a replica of Susan, diligent, domesticated, apparently free of selfish ambition. Presently I added, 'I'd rather like to have been there myself.'

She looked up questioningly. 'Where?'

'At the rehearsal. I've never attended one.'

'You'd find it a shambles,' She wasn't reacting with instant horror to the feeler, and I could guess why. In my enfeebled state, I wasn't wholly to be trusted to remain at home alone for an entire evening and relax, as ordered. It would take little, in Elaine's estimation, to lure me back to Fleet Street after dark to run a spot-check on the first editions. For the moment, every filial instinct in my younger daughter stood at red alert. Neutrally she added, 'You wouldn't really want to drag along?'

'Why not? I've only got to sit there.'

'If you came,' she said ponderously, like a parent laying down guidelines for the family treat, 'you'd have to promise me to stay quietly in your seat, not rush about trying to see everything, both sides of the curtain. You know what they said. You're not to overtax yourself.'

'Scout's honour,' I said meekly.

'Not only that—you're to stay incognito. I get enough ribbing as it is, over my Press connections. I don't want everyone pointing you out and looking meaningful.'

'I'm sure they'd never be so uncouth. There's just one thing . . .'

'Here it comes.'

'It's nothing. Only that there's someone else I'd like to have along. No, not Laura. Andy Kent, our latest recruit.

He's my other guest for the first night. A preview would fascinate him.'

'Let 'em all roll up,' she said wearily. 'If you flake out, he can carry you home.'

While Elaine was washing up in the kitchen, I put another call through to Planet House. The switchboard traced Andy to the file-room. I explained my idea. He said, 'You're keen to add to my theatrical education . . . or do you want me there in my strong-arm capacity? If so, you're backing a loser. You've not forgotten last night already?'

'You're too harsh on yourself, Andy.'

'Just realistic.'

'You did a good job, in the circumstances. I'd feel a lot happier tonight if you were around. Not that I really antici- pate trouble. This is a spur-of-the-moment idea, so unless my phone's being tapped . . . All the same, I'd like you to be there. Can you make it? We plan to leave here about six.'

'That gives me an hour. Are you driving yourself?'

'No, Elaine thinks I shouldn't. We thought of getting a Minicab.'

'I've a better idea. My own car's still in dock, but I can borrow one for the evening. I'll drive over and pick you both up.'

CHAPTER 18

As I had expected, Elaine and Andy got along famously. By the time we reached the street behind The Backstage where everyone parked, they were on terms of fairly ribald insult- swapping and I was having fatherly fantasies about the pair of them. The age-difference, I decided, was supremely unim- portant, particularly when compared with all the other, infinitely more stomach-turning differences that existed between Elaine and Jimmy Maxwell. Privately I laid plans for inviting Andy over to dinner. A spot of parental assistance, I reasoned, sometimes did nobody any harm.

The neighbourhood in which The Backstage had flourished for fifteen turbulent years was not, in touristic terms or indeed in any other terms that occurred to me, a showpiece of the capital. Set uncomfortably at the hub of a maze of streets between Islington and Shoreditch, the theatre, a converted warehouse, had made its way in spite rather than because of its environment, earning a reputation beyond its evident capacities by dint of the steadfast pursuit of anything deemed revolutionary in theatrical experience, and retaining the respect of hard-bitten national Press critics by the consistent standard of its productions. Almost anything The Backstage did was news. Although not by inclination a playgoer, I should have known this much even without Elaine as a daughter. The name could legitimately be mentioned in the same breath as a percentage of the West End establishments: there was even vague talk of new premises on a nearby site, to be funded with help from the Arts Council and the City. So far, it remained a pipedream.

Inside, Elaine delivered an ultimatum about keeping our heads down, and vanished. Finding our way into the auditorium, we claimed a couple of back-row seats—there was no circle—and watched a figure or two flit distractedly across the exposed stage, an elliptical affair which intruded so far into the front stalls that parts of the seating faced inwards at right-angles to the remainder. 'Theatre in the Semi-Round,' Andy observed knowledgeably. 'Still, they do run to a curtain.'

This was correct in a literal sense. Instead of rising and falling, the curtain hissed on curved runners from right to left: I wondered how exit lines survived its travel, which seemed shaky and uncertain to a fault. Two skeletal youths were testing it repeatedly, carrying out cryptic adjustments and chittering to each other. Someone else was experimenting with the sound effects system, producing ghostly roars and whistles over the amplifiers. In the midst of all this, the working team from the *Planet* arrived.

It comprised Paul Mellick from Features, and a photographer called Tim Atkinson whose speciality was new season's beachwear and lingerie. He brought a subtlety to the presentation of the female form that, I liked to think, had set new standards for the opposition to surpass. Laura made much use of him. His choice for this assignment had been inevitable. With a wave in our direction, the pair of them tramped down to stage level and consulted one of the emaciated youths, who pointed into the wings. They passed out of sight.

Andy produced a hip-flask. 'Care for a swig?'

'Why, do I look green?'

'I thought you might need a bracer. Waiting to see your own daughter on stage . . .'

'I should be used to it. I've watched her a few times. Never in rehearsal, though.'

Taking a mouthful from the flask, Andy replaced the cap and returned to a study of the curtain manœuvres. 'If it were me,' he said, 'I'd be paralysed.'

'With pride?'

'That might depend . . . What orders have you given our lensman down there?'

'It's not up to me, but I think I can guess the brief he's working to.'

'And it doesn't bother you?'

I hesitated. 'If it advances Elaine's career—as it should— I'm prepared to swallow a few scruples.' I gave him a wry glance. 'I'd be something of a hypocrite if I put up too much of a protest. We're publishing comparable pictures all the time . . . of other people's daughters.'

Andy nodded seriously. 'Can't fault your reasoning.' He

sat up. 'Looks like some action.'

Three people had wandered on to the stage, from which the curtain had finally lurched fully aside to vanish into the wings. Simultaneously, a familiar figure had shambled into the third row of the stalls and occupied a seat or two at one side, from which it examined broodingly the trio as they took up positions. Elaine, clad in a wisp of see-through nylon robe over bikini pants, planted herself on a wooden chair placed upstage, centre-right. An older woman, thickset and trousered, wearing spectacles, adopted a full-length posture on the boards at her right side and rested a cheek against a chairleg. The third member of the cast, a slim young man with deepset eyes and a great deal of bright yellow hair, swept across his scalp like wind-beaten corn, was garbed in black silk pyjamas with scarlet piping, and clutching a 'cello-case. Lowering the burden on to its edge, he sank on to the broader end and fell into an attitude of hopelessness.

'Action?' I muttered in an aside. 'You're living in the past, let me tell you.'

The older woman began to sing. Her voice was reedy, offkey, like a hacksaw blade drawn across stretched rubber bands. This went on for some while. It continued inexorably when the corn-haired young man leapt suddenly clear of the 'cello-case, kicked it violently to the rear of the stage, released a falsetto cry and then retired down-stage to rejoin it, dropping to a crouch with a hand on each clasp and becoming motionless, with his back to the audience.

The dirge expired. In the ensuing hush. Elaine leaned forward—at some expense to the hang of the nylon robe—to rumple the older woman's silver-streaked dark hair, causing its owner to stretch herself like a cat. Sliding down from the chair, Elaine joined her at floor-level. I held my breath.

Curling up alongside her companion, Elaine appeared to fall asleep. The woman lay on her spine and stared at the stage ceiling.

From the wings a middle-aged man drifted into view, carrying a small Jack Russell terrier. Planting the dog down behind the chair, he administered a gentle kick to its hind-quarters and it trotted off stage. He then took possession of the chair.

Rolling over in her sleep, Elaine came to rest on top of the woman, who ignored her.

Andy turned to me. 'Is this Scene One, or are they waiting for the—'

I quelled him with a gesture. Regardless of the fact that loyalty to Elaine would have gripped me in my seat whatever took place in front of our eyes, the rhythm of the proceedings was starting to get to me. Rick Smythe, I thought, might have economized on dialogue, but his stage directions must have filled sheets by the ream. The cast, to judge from their director's third-row passivity, was action-perfect. The next thing to happen was the opening of the 'cello-case by the young man and the revelation of, not a musical instrument, but a small female child dressed in a crinoline. Nursing her like a mother, he crooned into her ear between short, occasional outbursts of hysterical laughter. I began to feel sorry for the child until I realized that she was an inflatable dummy. Then I felt sorry for the young man, until he kicked her away out of sight and sat inside the 'cello-case himself to glare into space. After that I started hoping that Jimmy Maxwell would find it necessary to intervene.

When he finally did, it seemed to be at the conclusion of Act One . . . or, as Elaine had explained, the first play of the pair. No particular event to mark the finish was discernible, except that the cast came collectively to their feet and stood waiting in heedful stances while the hunchbacked figure of the director swarmed agilely on to the stage and began prowling as though in search of missing scenery. From the wings, Paul Mellick appeared with cassette tape-recorder held at the ready: behind him, Tim Atkinson lurked with his camera, taking a quick shot of Maxwell as he came to rest with a foot on the chair and his chin supported by a palm held in place by his knee. The cast shuffled uneasily.

Removing her spectacles, the thickset woman said on a note of resentment, 'Okay, we missed it that time.'

'Honestly, Jimmy,' put in the young man, 'it's a *swine* to catch hold of. The *projectional* problems . . . Elaine, love, how do you feel about it?'

Restored to a semblance of decency, Elaine said placidly, 'I find I'm burrowing into it now. You have to take it at its own pace. Let it breathe.'

'Discussion later,' Maxwell said tersely. 'We've got Mr Mellick here, from the *Planet.* He'd like to . . .' Vaguely he brandished a paw.

Mellick stepped forward, closer to Elaine than I deemed strictly necessary for his purpose. 'A part like this, Miss Rodgers, must present something of a challenge. What's been your method of approach?'

'Instinct,' she told him, with a professional smile. 'We've all had to rely on a sort of gut-feeling about what's involved. There's really no other way.'

Mellick nodded earnestly, moved a pace nearer in a pretence of embracing the others with his survey. 'Anyone like to tell me what the play's *about*?'

'Loneliness,' explained Elaine.

'A political statement,' said the older woman, replacing her glasses.

'What kind of a statement?'

While they were all launching forth, Maxwell conferred in an undertone with Tim Atkinson, who presently took command. Sequences of the play were re-run patiently by the cast to provide shots: all of them featured in Atkinson's programme, but the emphasis upon Elaine and her sartorial disarray was noticeable, and mentally I cringed at the thought of Monday's issue. To take my mind off it I turned back to Andy, who seemed to be engaged in a little theme-analysis on his own account, and getting nowhere. 'What,' I inquired, 'was your reaction to that?'

His smile gave nothing away. 'I might ask you the same.'

'Mine was fatherly.'

'In the applauding sense?'

'Don't tie me down. I just hope all this does Elaine a bit of good, career-wise. She works damned hard.'

'Also she's very attractive,' he said, watching Mellick. 'She may have to watch her step.'

'She's pretty cagey. No need,' I said, as an experiment, 'to worry too much on her behalf. She seems to have things under control, at the moment.'

No visible reaction came from Andy. We sat in silence, watching the camera session on stage reach a conclusion while Maxwell loped from point to point like a zoo creature at feeding time, clearly impatient to rinse the *Planet* out of his hair and get back to the real business of dismembering the performances. Presently Andy spoke again. 'Rick Smythe isn't here, I take it?'

'Unlikely. He prefers to keep well clear until opening night, Elaine tells me.'

'So that's Jimmy Maxwell, the director?'

'Right.'

Andy's gaze once more became fixed. Easing myself back in the seat, I tried to rest my head, which was threatening to readmit a throb or two. Closing my eyes, I listened dreamily to the various sounds bouncing around the theatre, wishing I was home in bed. Presently I heard Andy's voice. He was murmuring something I hadn't quite caught the gist of. My eyes snapped open.

'What was that?'

'I said, it's a funny thing, but the way that Maxwell character moves . . .' His voice tailed off.

'Like a caged leopard,' I agreed. 'What about it?'

'It's probably just a coincidence . . .'

'Andy, what the blazes are you getting at?'

'I'm not sure,' he said slowly. 'But here's one thing I can tell you. It's remarkably like the movement I glimpsed in the alley last night, just before you were hit.'

CHAPTER 19

At two in the morning, I lay dragging on a slim cigar in the silence of my bedroom, striving to lay out my thoughts in a pattern that made some kind of sense.

On the way home, Elaine had been on an artistic high. 'That second time, we really hit it,' she kept saying. 'Suddenly it all seemed to drop into place. Did you notice? Just after Steve comes on with the dog . . . We'd been having such problems there, Janice and me, but tonight . . . How did it strike you,' she demanded trustingly, 'from where you were sitting?'

I gave her hand a squeeze. 'No comparison, the second time around.'

'Isn't it weird? For weeks you give it all you've got, without getting a spark. Then without any warning . . . I can't explain it. Nobody can. You just know when you've crashed the barrier.'

Although, in my view, the second run-through had varied in no perceptible respect from the first, I had no plans to hint as much. 'Jimmy was pleased, then?'

'I wouldn't put it as high as that. Slightly mollified. Yesterday evening I thought he was going to throw a fit. Lucky for us he had to leave early.'

My fingers tightened again, involuntarily this time, on hers. 'Why was that?'

'He went to visit his brother,' explained Elaine. 'He

always gets a bit temperamental beforehand. I gather his brother can be difficult.'

From the wheel, Andy said idly across his shoulder, 'Where does he live?'

'The brother? Hammersmith. He's in a sheltered block of bedsits for the partially disabled.'

'How does Jimmy get there? By Tube?'

'No, he takes the car. If his brother feels up to it, he can run him down to the local for a quick one.'

'Must be awkward,' I remarked, 'packing a disabled person into a Mini.'

'Oh, Jimmy's got a different car now. Didn't I tell you? A silver-grey Maestro. Very swish.'

'I think I may have spotted it outside the apartment. The new "B" registration, right? Let's think ... B319 ... RH ...'

'No use trying to show off your giant memory, Dad. You've got the wrong car. Jimmy's is A427 SLV. Learning lines,' she said smugly, 'is good practice for remembering numbers, too.'

'We're impressed,' said Andy. 'But how's your memory for other things? Bet you can't tell us how many rehearsals you've missed in the past few weeks through Jimmy's absence.'

'Around half a dozen,' she replied promptly. 'But that's no fault of his. He does have other commitments. Which makes his dedication all the more impressive, if you ask me. This is why we bust our guts for him. I get so sick when I feel we've let him down. Which explains why we were getting rattled, all of us, over this new piece. That first section, we just couldn't seem to grab it . . . it kept sliding off in different . . .'

For the rest of the journey we had let Elaine hold the stage happily, re-living the triumph of the rehearsal and speculating upon the likely content of Monday's *Planet*, to the prurient interest of which she had evidently become fully reconciled. Still euphoric on reaching home, she had invited Andy in for a nightcap: to my private relief he had declined and driven off with a straight-faced look in my direction, remarking only that he would be in touch. Inside the apartment, Elaine did a twirl about the living-room, shedding outer garments, before remembering that I was an invalid and must be packed off to bed in case I keeled over from a relapse. 'Tomorrow morning,' she commanded, 'you're to lie in until I call you. How do you feel?'

'All right, physically. Elaine, there's something—'

'I'll bring you breakfast in bed, and then you must promise me to spend the morning doing *absolutely nothing* as hard as you can. You're still looking a little pale.'

'Put it down to fatherly excitement.' Taking both her hands, I drew her closer and stood looking down at her flushed, animated face, seeing Susan in her expression so forcibly that I had to pause and take a quick breath before resuming. 'Now that you've cracked Act One,' I said speculatively, 'or Play the First, or whatever the damn thing's officially called . . . maybe you can all let up a bit? At least you'll get the weekend off?'

'You're joking!' Elaine landed a kiss of daughterly admonishment upon my jawline. 'We'll be going at it harder than ever. If you produced a newspaper chockful of scoops, you wouldn't forget about tomorrow's issue, would you? Not,' she appended hastily, 'when you were feeling well, that is. It's the same in the theatre. We'll be back on stage tomorrow afternoon, getting bawled at, don't you worry.'

'Afternoon? So you'll be home in the evening?'

'Actually, no,' she said, regarding me dubiously. 'Jimmy's had an invite to a last-night party from a mate of his.'

'Ah. You'll be late, then.'

'Well, it doesn't start till after the final performance. But I expect we shan't stay long.'

'Where is it?'

'On-stage at the Open House, in Hackney. You'll be all right, left to yourself?'

'I shan't throw a wild bash of my own here, if that's what you mean. Question is, my dear, will *you* be all right? After a strenuous stint of rehearsals . . .'

She punched me lightly on the chest. 'What you're really saying is—Hackney, after dark! Simmer down, Dad. Jimmy takes as good care of me as a maiden aunt. We'll simply drive there, attend the party, then drive home. No problem.'

'That's okay, then.' I paused for a second. 'It's nice, I suppose, to be with someone you've total faith in.'

'It does save a lot of hassle. No emotional involvement, either,' Elaine said carelessly. 'Is that what you're worried about? No need to be. It's all so platonic, it's almost insulting. Suits me, though. I wouldn't want to get into anything heavy, just now.' She stood on tiptoe to kiss me properly. 'Sleep tight. We want you in fighting trim by Monday.'

A sleepless night, I reflected, stubbing out the cigar, was no preparation for such an objective. Thumping the pillows into shape, I lay down in a new posture and applied myself grimly to the search for repose. I had come to a decision.

'Me, too,' said Andy. After an interval he added, 'You don't think maybe we're getting fanciful?'

'I don't see we can afford to be anything else. Candidly, I'd sooner chase a rainbow than take a chance. How about it, then? I know it's Saturday, but could you do that for me?'

'You want me to start compiling a dossier on the guy. Lifestyle, background . . . the works.'

'You've got it. And I'd be grateful if you could work fast.'

A mirthless laugh came down the line. Behind his voice I could hear another, the controlled gabble of a TV or radio presenter; there were also the faint sounds of water boiling and a cat mewling. 'You know how I enjoy a challenge,' he said ironically. 'I can see the urgency, but don't expect miracles. It's a question of making a start . . .'

'How about that registration number? SLV isn't so far removed from "an S and a W". The lad who spotted the car in the clearing could easily have slipped up over a detail like that.'

'Sure. I'll look into it.'

'Then there's the brother at Hammersmith. Did he in fact receive a visit on Thursday evening? If so, between what times?'

'Got you. And the theatrical costumiers?'

'They're definitely worth a check. Where do they accommodate their girl typist? Could that Laski portable have been accessible to a customer at any time? Have they recently had dealings with . . . you get my drift?'

The click of a switch cut off the sound of hissing water. 'I've made a note of all that,' Andy said presently, as though returning to the phone from a tour of the kitchen. 'I'll call you the moment I—ouch! Get off, you little ruffian. Sorry. Nikki the kitten was just testing his claws on my left foot. I'll give him some breakfast, then push right on with inquiries. It may be this evening before I'm in a position to call back. Is that soon enough?'

'It'll have to be.' I stared unhappily through the window at the buildings opposite. Hearing footsteps, I added quickly, 'Do what you can,' and hung up before he could reply.

'Who was that?' Elaine inquired sleepily, appearing in night attire at the living-room door.

'Wally Farr, my news editor.'

'He doesn't want you there?' she demanded suspiciously.

'Relax. It was just an admin query.'

'He shouldn't be pestering you with it.' Yawning, she headed for the kitchen. 'If I don't have a coffee-fix, I'll go into convulsions.' At the doorway she turned, focused upon me with an effort. 'Chipper this morning? No reaction from last night?'

'Virtually back to normal.' I gave her a relaxed beam. The half-truths were starting to come easily: too easily. Wandering after her, I watched her while she blindly clawed cups and coffee jars from wall-racks. 'If it's reaction we're talking about,' I remarked presently, 'you're the one who should be suffering. The artistic tension was all yours. Sure you want to flog along to this party tonight?'

'No, I couldn't care less about it.' She primed the cups with instant granules. 'I'm only going to keep Jimmy company. He's not wild about celebrations. It's only loyalty to this pal of his . . .' She fumbled in a drawer for teaspoons.

'I should have thought you could have both given it a miss.'

'We won't stay long.' Clattering a spoon into each saucer, she turned to regard me in a puzzled way. 'You're a proper old fusspot, all of a sudden. I've told you, haven't I? When I'm with Jimmy there's no need to worry, he's as strong as an ox and he looks after me like a mother-hen. We don't . . .' Pausing, she studied me more intently. 'You don't like the thought of being here by yourself? Is that it?'

'Don't be absurd, Elaine.'

'It's perfectly understandable,' she continued, as if I hadn't spoken. 'An attack like that can rock a person's confidence. And you don't feel a hundred per cent yet, do you? I can see you don't. Look, while I'm gone, why don't you ask Laura to come round? She'd jump at it. Then you could—'

'I don't need a home guardian,' I said desperately. 'I'm perfectly happy to stay here alone. It's nothing to do with that. All I'm concerned about . . .'

'What?' she prompted, as I hesitated.

'I just don't want you overdoing things,' I finished feebly. 'You can, you know, even at your age.'

Flashing me a grin, she turned back to plug in the kettle. 'I'll bear it in mind, you poor old thing.'

After breakfast Elaine went out to shop for a few essentials, having first elicited from me a pledge that I should be staying indoors to pull abreast of some personal correspondence and nurse my remaining bruises. After she had gone, as a salve to my conscience I did scrawl a letter or two—one of them inevitably to Katie, expressing contrition for having reduced our tiff to the level of public farce and hoping this would not rule out an eventual amnesty, on her terms—before dialling Laura's home number, which was engaged. No sooner had I hung up than my own telephone shrilled. The caller was Laura. I said, 'I was just trying to get you.'

'Oh!' She sounded pleased. 'I didn't want to ring too early, in case you were still sleeping it off. How do you feel?'

'Largely from memory. No, not true. I'm in fair shape, thanks. In myself.'

'What does that mean? Outside yourself you're a gibbering wreck?'

'I've one or two things on my mind.'

'If it's *Planet* matters you're uptight about, forget 'em. When I left last night, everything was muddling along as usual. It will, you know. Wally Farr and the other—'

'I know. I sweat too much. Actually, though, I'm not too concerned about the people minding the shop. It's something more personal.'

'Still no word from Katie?' she said immediately. 'Little wretch. She might have relented by now. Lucky you're friends with Elaine again. That is, she seemed very solicitous about you on Thursday night, so I assume . . . Or has she backslid since?'

'No no, everything's fine between us. There's only one thing, Laura, that I should mention. Regarding next Thursday . . .'

'Elaine's first night at The Backstage?'

'Yes. Things are slightly in the air at present.'

'No seats available?'

'I've got the tickets. No problem there.'

'But it may be delayed? Rehearsals gone haywire?'

'Nothing like that. There's just a faint question-mark . . . All I'm saying is, don't cancel any rival engagement that may come up in the meantime, okay?'

'What's this?' she asked brightly. 'A polite shove-off?'

'Christ, no.' I sat cursing myself. 'Don't get the wrong impression. All I meant was, should you get an offer that sounds inviting, don't pass it up for the sake of . . . Oh hell. Come to dinner that evening anyway.'

'You're on. I hope we can round it off with a theatre trip, but if we can't I'll survive.' A little breathlessly she added, 'Take things easy, Peter, over the weekend. See you Monday, back on form.' Without awaiting a reply she rang off.

For a few minutes I sat thinking of her. Few women, I imagined, would have taken my verbal fumbling so equably, ended the conversation so precisely at the right time and on the right note. I felt a passing though acute regret that I hadn't followed Elaine's suggestion and asked Laura round for that evening. If I happened to change my mind, there was still time to rectify the omission. Meanwhile, I had letters to post. A stroll to the postbox hardly counted as a breach of my undertaking to remain indoors. Stamping the envelopes, I travelled by lift to street level and for an exhilarating three hundred yards doused myself in the spring sunshine that was spreading a coat of pale gold over everything in sight; then, instead of turning back, I went on, continued around the block. I needed the exercise. It was the only way to clear my head, get my thoughts into some kind of order.

Among other things, I was trying to take a detached look at what I felt about Laura, plus a realistic one at what she might feel about me. It was a fair time since I had given serious consideration to any woman, other than Susan. In a sense, I had mislaid the knack. Musings of this nature had become such a novelty that I needed time, and the right circumstances, in which to give them the attention they demanded. Present circumstances were far from right. Other things were blocking my mental view. Reluctantly I switched over to them.

How about a subterfuge?

I could pretend, after lunch, to be feeling suddenly worse. In her concern for me, Elaine would have no hesitation in ditching her plans for the rest of the day. The idea was tempting, but after probing it from all sides I knew that it must be abandoned. To feign illness would have led to stupefying complications: I doubted whether I could have carried it off.

Another appeal to her native prudence? *Elaine, the pace is getting too much for you. Slow down, before you blow your chances.* Or an assertion of parental authority? *Elaine, you're to get an early night. No argument. It's vital if you're to do justice to yourself . . .*

Nothing was practicable. Elaine had gone her own way too long for me to put the process suddenly into reverse. Anything I said would raise her hackles, be counter-productive. With an inner groan, I completed the circuit of the block and returned to the apartment, which closed in around me again like a jailhouse. I toyed with the notion of calling Laura, putting the invitation to her: something held me back. Stretching out on the couch instead, I sipped a weak brandy and tried to lose myself in the newspapers. They seemed much less absorbing than usual.

On Elaine's return with the groceries, I made a final effort.

'Andy may be calling over this evening.'

'Good,' she said abstractedly, stowing frozen vegetables in the freezer. 'Company for you.'

'Pity you won't be here.'

'Why?'

'He'd like to have seen you,' I said in desperation.

'How do you know?'

'I think he was knocked out by you last night.'

Slamming the freezer door, Elaine emitted a small shriek. 'He didn't make it very obvious. Wouldn't even venture inside for a drink. Climb off it, Dad. I'm not the type to turn men's heads in half an hour.'

'That,' I informed her, 'shows how little you know about yourself . . . or about men, for that matter.'

'Okay,' she said good-humouredly. 'I'm dead ignorant, and happy with it. Meanwhile you can stop trying to act Cupid. I'm the performer of this outfit, remember.'

'As if I could forget.' I sat observing her for a while. I knew when I was licked. 'Enjoy the party,' I added presently. 'If you've reason to think Jimmy's over the alcohol limit, give us a buzz. I can always drive out and bring you both back.'

'You're to stop indoors and *rest*.' Elaine eyed me with a faint frown. 'Anyway, Jimmy never drinks more than a glass at a time. You do seem to be flapping about things, all of a sudden.'

'Delayed shock,' I explained. 'Take no notice. Just look after yourself, and have a good time.'

CHAPTER 20

The call from Andy came through shortly after ten.

There was no mistaking the urgency in his voice. 'Can you get out here right away? It's important.'

My stomach gave a lurch. 'Where are you?'

'Hackney. Near the Open House Theatre. Maxwell has just driven up with Elaine.'

I said faintly, 'You think she's in danger?'

'I'm not certain. I've things to tell you about him, but

you'd better get along here first. I'll explain later.'

'Tell me where you want us to meet.'

As I thrust my way through the first set of doors into The Bricklayer's Arms, my progress was blocked. Andy, in zipped brown leather jacket and with an air of tension about him, restrained me with a hand on my shoulder while nodding towards the street. 'No time,' he said, 'for a quiet chat at the bar. Let's get back outside.'

'Is Elaine all right?'

'For the moment, I'm sure. But I suggest we don't waste any time.' Reaching the footway, he glanced across the street at the faintly-lit façade of the Open House Theatre, then turned his attention to the nearside kerb. 'Where did you leave your car?'

I indicated where it stood with two wheels on the pavement. He said, 'I've parked mine in a back street, out of sight. For the time being I plan to leave it there.' He strode out briskly for the Cavalier, leaving me to follow. In my haste I had left the doors unlocked. Letting himself into the front passenger seat, he shut himself inside and waited for me to join him. 'I suppose you're wondering what the hell this is all about?'

'The thought did cross my mind. What is it you've dug up regarding—'

'There's really no time for that, just now.' Half-turned in the seat, he was observing the Open House steadfastly, as if on the alert for the smallest deviation from its apparent lifelessness. 'They're both in there,' he added, slipping a small peppermint into his mouth. 'The audience left about an hour ago. Soon after that, Maxwell and Elaine bowled up in his Maestro—it's parked just round the corner—and went inside. That's when I called you.'

'How long have you been here?'

'Long enough to work up an appetite.' He crunched

noisily into the peppermint. 'But I think I may have achieved something. Give me a little more time and I'll elucidate. First, I'd like to make a suggestion.'

'What is it?'

'That you walk over there, get inside, gatecrash that party and ask Elaine and Maxwell to leave with you . . . immediately.'

'Both of them?'

'Yes, that's vital. Make sure Maxwell comes too.'

'Won't he think it odd?'

'Let him think what he likes. How you do it doesn't matter: just get the pair of them out of there and into this car. Tell Elaine there's bad news about Katie. Anything, but fetch her.'

'Maxwell will want to get her back into his own car.'

'Don't let him. Devise some story that'll induce him to come with us. You'll realize the importance when I've had time to explain.'

I sat drumming the wheel. My mind had been wiped clean, injected with a numbing dose. 'I can't think of a yarn to pitch them . . .'

'You'll manage. Just get inside there and start talking.'

He gave me an encouraging prod. Like a cub reporter on his first assignment, I clambered out of the car and walked on wobbly knees across a street that seemed to have stretched to a width of a thousand yards, towards a theatre foyer that looked as if it had never been in touch with living people. Approaching a side door, I could see a bulb or two glowing inside; that was all. Hopelessly I tried the door. To my astonishment it swung inwards to admit me into the stuffy interior. A choice of inner doors confronted me. Selecting the nearest, I went through.

A buzz of voices and a chinking of bottles became audible. A side-aisle took me down to the stage area, which was curtained off in more traditional style than that of The

Backstage and on the extreme right was equipped with a short flight of steps leading to a narrow door. Another push got me through.

The party was taking place on stage, inside a representation of an attic room with a staircase leading up and out to nowhere. Over to the left, a makeshift bar had been set up with the aid of furniture from the production: close by, a card-table bore paper plates of sausage rolls and biscuits. Twenty or thirty people were standing around, consuming and conversing. Music pulsed softly from the address system. At my appearance, one or two incurious glances strayed my way: nobody asked who I was. At the rear of the stage, a mass of coppery tresses stood out, glinting under the lights and reflected in a wall-mirror. With a sense of overpowering relief, I saw that Elaine was looking well and cheerful, eating a sausage roll and chatting spiritedly to a tall man of indeterminate years who seemed to be treating her with deference. Of Maxwell there was no sign. My stomach began to unravel. Threading my way across, I stood waiting for a chance to intervene. Elaine spotted me first.

'Dad! What on earth—'

The predictability of the inquiry served as a lubricant. Without hesitation I said gravely, 'Sorry, darling, to butt in. Slight emergency, I'm afraid. Katie rang.'

'Yes?' she said apprehensively.

'Might I have a word in private?' I gave the tall man a smile of apology. Waving both arms in a larger-than-life gesture of self-exclusion and forgiveness, he took himself off to a neighbouring group. I drew Elaine aside. 'Actually,' I told her, detesting myself, 'it wasn't Katie herself who called. It was someone on her behalf. She seems to have met with an accident of some kind, though it's not clear—'

Elaine's horrified gasp cut into my words. 'Oh no! Is it bad? Has she—'

'I don't know the details. I think,' I said desperately, 'she's going to be all right, but I've an address for us to go to and we ought to leave right now. Is Jimmy around?'

She looked distractedly about the set. 'He was here a moment ago. I'll leave a message. My coat . . .'

'No, don't do that. Find him, will you? He's needed, too.'

'Jimmy?' She gazed at me uncomprehendingly. 'What does it have to do with him? He doesn't even know Katie.'

'His strength may come in useful.'

Partial insight flashed into Elaine's pupils. 'Is Katie trapped somewhere? They need someone who can—'

'Just find him, darling. I'll wait here.'

She hurried off into the wings. Seeing me alone, the tall man gravitated back towards me, this time in company with a pert girl who gave me a toothsome smile and announced, 'Gerry tells me you're Elaine's old man. Bet you're proud. She's landed herself a lulu of a—'

Elaine darted back with Maxwell in tow. 'Right, let's go,' she panted, hauling him past us. Maxwell, clad in a thick-knit sweater and corduroys, looked bemused but compliant. I raised a hand in another apology.

'I'm sorry, we have to—'

'Dad, you're wasting time!' Elaine and the director were already out of sight beyond the curtain. Sprinting in pursuit, I caught up with them in the foyer.

'Car's across the street. I've got Andy with me.'

'You go,' Maxwell told Elaine. 'I'll follow in mine.'

'No—it'll be quicker if you come with us.'

He gave me a puzzled stare. I grabbed his arm: beneath the man-made fibre it felt muscular, steel-hard, trunk-thick. 'We can pick yours up later. If you travel separately, you might lose us.'

With a shrug, he accompanied us over to the Cavalier. Jumping out of the front seat, Andy beckoned to Elaine. 'You and I sit in the back,' he suggested, holding open the door. 'Mr Maxwell can help your father to navigate. His eyesight's probably better than mine.'

It was smoothly done. I was less enchanted by the proximity at my left shoulder of the hunchbacked figure of the director as, at Andy's direction, I drove to the next intersection and turned right. Behind me, Elaine said in a voice half-strangled by suppressed dread, 'Who was it rang, Dad? Someone we know?'

With as much conviction as I could muster, I shook my head. 'Total stranger to me. He didn't give his name.'

'What did he *say*, exactly?'   .

'Asked if I was Katie's father. Said she was in trouble and could we bring some help.'

'What kind of trouble?'

'He was cagey on that.'

'Hadn't he tried dialling nine-nine-nine?'

'He seemed to want it kept from the authorities.'

A moan escaped from Elaine. 'What in the world has Katie been up to? Is it far?'

Andy said quietly, 'We'll be there in less than an hour.'

'An *hour?*'

Raising his voice a little, he addressed me. 'If you follow this road as far as the roundabout, I'll direct you again. It's a forty limit,' he added helpfully, 'for the next mile. After that you can step on it.'

As near as I could gauge, we were heading north-east out of London. The hypothesis was confirmed when we reached the roundabout, a giant affair with roads striking off in all directions and a superfluity of signs to bemuse the traveller. Andy spoke up again. 'Bear left . . . here. That's it. Now keep straight ahead.'

'Where are we aiming for?' Elaine demanded in a choked voice. 'What's Katie doing in this—'

'Better let your father concentrate,' Andy advised, not unkindly.

It was hard not to turn round, send her a note of comfort.

Common sense kept me facing rigidly to the front. As things stood, Elaine was giving a performance of total conviction: anything less would have been sniffed out by Maxwell with the ease of a dog scenting raw meat. For my part, silence was the obvious ploy. The anxious father, hugging his fears to himself. The scenario, in truth, was not so far from reality. My mental confusion was severe enough to keep me speech-less.

Patches of woodland began to appear on each side of the highway, illuminated by the headlamps of the traffic both ways. Any remaining doubts as to our location were dis-pelled. The same realization had seeped through to Elaine. 'Surely,' she said wretchedly from the rear seat, 'this must be Epping Forest? Why on earth—'

'Take the next turn-off to the left,' put in Andy. 'Then keep on for half a mile.'

'Katie never mentioned she was coming here,' wailed Elaine.

I spotted my chance. 'Where did she tell you she was staying?'

'With Laurence in Hampstead. That's what she said. Why would they want to come out to Epping Forest?'

Laurence of Hampstead. A fresh name to me. Manifestly, however, it wasn't to Elaine, and this involuntary exposure of her mild treachery to me on behalf of her sister took some of the heat out of my present compassion for her, although I knew that sibling loyalty had been her sole motive. Smouldering a little, I eased the car into the left-hand turn and flicked the headlamps to main beam.

We were now on a B-road, well-metalled but narrow, coal-dark, stifled on each flank by a screen of trees. At the instant of our leaving the main highway, traffic had dropped away abruptly to nothing. The digital clock on the panel indicated that it was nearly midnight.

After a mile or two the road surface became uneven,

causing the car to pitch a little, nudging Maxwell forward spasmodically in his seat against the harness. His movements gave the disquieting impression that he was trying to butt a hole in the windscreen with his forehead. I throttled back.

'You'll see a gap in the trees shortly,' volunteered Andy. 'Offside, a few hundred yards. Take us in there.'

Sounding a little hysterical, Elaine said, 'How do you know just where to go? Did Laurence explain all this?'

Andy remained diplomatically silent. I could guess the sequence of events. He had been here already, earlier in the day, in quest of . . . just exactly what? The fact that he had been able to rediscover the spot so unerringly suggested that he had spent some time in the vicinity. With some fervour, I hoped he had taken all possible dangers into account. The four of us were now in small-hours isolation in the centre of nowhere. Slowing further, I peered ahead, alert for an opening.

'There it is,' said Andy.

The Cavalier gave a bounce or two as I took it across the verge on to leaf-mould and roots. I heard a gasp from Elaine. At walking pace I rolled the car forward, peering for signs of a track, a gateway. The gap narrowed. Tree-trunks crowded us: a squelching of mud announced itself beneath the tyres.

'I don't think we can go much further . . .'

'Right,' said Andy. 'Handbrake on, and you'd better douse the lights.'

Gingerly I carried out both instructions. If Maxwell was planning a move, now was the instant for him to make it. When Andy spoke again there was no detectable tension in his voice. 'Okay, we've arrived. How's this for a Godforsaken corner of the earth? For the moment, I suggest we all stay in the car. Go ahead, Elaine. You can tell them now.'

A spell of silence followed. The rear-view mirror showed

me nothing: it was too dark. Alongside me, Maxwell seemed to be contorting himself slightly, as if trying to swivel his body so that he could direct his gaze past the neck-restraints towards the rear seats. Presently Elaine's voice came out of the blackness. A different voice, lower-pitched, on a level key.

'Dad . . . he's holding me. I can't move.'

'That's all right, my dear.' I spoke lightly, reassuringly, hoping the anodyne reply was appropriate. Unbriefed, I was having to improvise. 'Nothing to worry about.'

As my pupils adjusted to the dense gloom, outlines were starting to consolidate. Maxwell, I could now perceive, had attained a semi-lateral position so that his head was fully turned towards the rear: I heard the stealthiest of clicks as he released his seat-belt. Every sinew I possessed tautened. Fear urged me to fire the engine, reverse out of the clearing, drive off furiously . . . anything to regain the initiative. Somehow I held myself in check. This wasn't my show. I had to go along with the schedule.

Maxwell seemed content to wait. His breathing was just audible. It sounded regular, untroubled. My own lungs were in suspension, awaiting the signal to restart.

'I rather think, Elaine,' remarked Andy, 'you'd better tell them again. Spell it out.'

'He's . . . got something up against my throat. Feels like a knife.'

'Correct. So the smallest movement on your daughter's part, Mr Rodgers . . . You're getting the message?'

'The situation needs clarifying.' My voice emerged hoarsely, which was a nuisance. Striving to be helpful, I was having to grope.

'Seems plain enough to me,' Andy said conversationally. 'Take off the blinkers, that's my advice.' There was a brief pause. 'But then, I suppose that's partly the problem. You don't know how.' A dry laugh came out of the darkness. 'Like a great many others. Which explains why so many are dispensable.'

Maxwell remained motionless. He seemed to be listening intently.

'To be perfectly honest,' Andy resumed without heat, 'I can't think why one should bother talking to you. Why not simply put you out of harm's way, same as the others? Easy, Elaine . . . Steady, my precious. You're not on the list. I wouldn't do that. Not unless I had to.'

'What is it you want to say to us, Andy?' My brain was starting to advance in jerks, like a corroded clockwork mouse across a roughened floor.

'First, I'd like Elaine to give you another caution. Go ahead, Elaine.'

'He means it. Don't try anything.'

'Smart girl. I'm sure our listeners are picking up the message.'

The clockwork mouse gave a sudden surge. In my relief I almost gave a shout of laughter. Self-control was necessary. Unlike Elaine, I was about to make my debut as a performer: the attempt had to be good.

'All right, Kent. You win.' A lifeless monotone. The effect wasn't altogether negligible: I felt rather pleased with it. 'You had everybody fooled, all along. Why don't you tell us the details?'

CHAPTER 21

The forest lay stiller than death.

Behind the tail-end of the car, the lane remained cocooned in hushed darkness. There were no night-sounds, no screechings, no rustlings in the thickets. If anything was alive out there, it was holding its breath.

'Neither of you,' said Andy, 'lacks imagination. Why don't you try working it out for yourselves?'

'I'm a newspaper man, not a detective.'

'A *Fleet Street* man.' He placed heavy emphasis upon the distinction. 'Training enough, I should have thought. In your position, you have to spend your life working things out. Eh, Rodgers? Putting yourself into people's minds and souls. Visualizing what might appeal to them . . . the lowest common factor that'll sell newspapers. Terribly good at that, aren't you, Rodgers? A real high-flyer.'

Under cover of the darkness I winced. He was scraping raw flesh. 'I do my best for the *Planet*'s shareholders, if that's what you mean. Is this relevant?'

'Only to the extent that it explains why parasites like yourselves have to be eliminated. Taken out of harm's way. It's our one chance.'

Back on track with him, I gave careful thought to the phrasing of the next question. 'This accounts for it, then. Why you had to dispose of John Wallington and Mel Winters . . . and before them, Paul Lewis and Carl Scott. All of them prostituting their talents, pandering to the grosser instincts of the human race—is that it?'

'The great thing about being in journalism,' said Andy, with apparent inconsequence, 'is that nobody ever questions your movements. Think about it. As long as you're on assignment—or even if you're not—you can go pretty well anywhere, any time, without exciting comment.'

I thought about it. 'So Wallington and the rest of them,' I ventured, 'presented no problem. At the time, you were working for the agency. Simple. You knew what was going on. People's habits, their engagements . . . their movements. All you had to do—'

'It wasn't that easy.' He sounded resentful. 'Lewis, yes. He was straightforward enough. But then he was a creature of routine. He always used that footway, same time every night.

All I had to do . . . A couple of seconds, that's what it took. As for the others . . .'

'Tell us,' I prompted, as he stopped.

'Winters—he was a challenge. I had to do a major research job on him. Luckily I'd got a footing with that Caroline of his—she imagined I was going to give her some publicity, the little fool, so she kept in with me—and one day she let slip about his visit to his dad. That provided the opportunity. Even then it was no cakewalk. He might have been a little guy, but he still took some heaving over that barrier. And then the concrete slabs might easily have missed . . . Hold still, Elaine. I don't want to hurt you.'

'Let her go, Kent. She's done nothing.'

'Some of us might dispute that. She's done a good bit already to help spread the rot . . . and I've no doubt she'd go on doing it, given the encouragement. It's not her fault. She's been led, strung along, just like . . .'

The sentence slurred away. For a moment Andy was silent, before adding quietly, 'Those misguiding her, and all the others like her . . . they've plenty to answer for. And answer they will, believe me. I'll see to it.'

Throughout this exchange, not a word or a movement had come from Maxwell. He seemed to have been iced into immobility. His nearness to me was petrifying, and yet at the same time I felt a crazy elation, almost a wish to find out just how far we could go along the taunting path we had embarked upon. Now fully in tune with Andy's strategy, I had no doubt of my ability to keep in step with the rhythm. Only the outcome remained in question. But we were committed now. There was no turning back.

'To an extent,' I remarked thoughtfully, 'I can understand your feelings, Andy, towards people like Mel Winters and Paul Lewis. It's arguable that they were helping to add to the sum of human corruption. But the Governor?'

'You're not using that imagination of yours.' Andy

sounded a little fatigued, as if tiring of explanations. 'As owner of the *Planet*, he was responsible for its gutter policy. It made sense to get rid of him, see whether any deck-swabbing occurred afterwards. Of course, it was too much to hope for. Things got worse. I'd miscalculated about you, Rodgers. Improvement? I soon saw which way the wind blew. You not only sanctioned that filth they're going to write about your daughter here . . . you welcomed it. A boost to her career. That's all that counts, isn't it? Getting her name in lights, coining the loot as it drips off her . . .'

His voice disappeared in a choke. When he resumed, it was on a calmer note.

'How you, as a father, could permit such a thing, let alone endorse it, is something I . . . But you did. And that's why you're here tonight, along with Maxwell. You had your chance. You blew it.'

'You're as bad. What made you think eliminating the Governor would alter things? You must be incredibly naive.'

'He didn't deserve to live, anyhow. He was better gone.'

'You had a lot of luck,' I said contemptuously. 'It was a muddled operation that could easily have misfired.'

'Muddled?' Andy took in a distinctly audible breath. 'If you recall, you yourself were the one who was obliging enough to describe his routine. The day you were dining with him—remember? I drove down to Hampshire to interview Carl Scott's brother. Coming back, I'd plenty of time. Time to make the detour to that Surrey mausoleum of his. Time to walk from where I'd left the car. Time to wait inside the boundary fence until he came along. Afterwards, all I had to do was stroll back to the car, stow the wheelbrace out of sight and drive home. Simple, but effective.'

'Most. Pity about the boy spotting your Escort.'

'No great harm done. He only got part of the registration. The full lettering, by the way, is WPS. How many light-coloured Escorts with similar numbers are there, dodging around in the South-East? Still, I took precautions. I've kept the car under cover at home ever since, and used that borrowed one. No sense in inviting trouble. Keep quite still, Elaine. I'd hate you to be hurt, even by accident.'

Still no movement from Maxwell. An insane impulse to press things to a conclusion brought words out of me in a tumble.

'What you're saying, Kent, makes sense—up to a point. But it does leave a few questions. If what I was doing repelled you so much, why did you agree to act as my bodyguard the other night? Why not let me be mugged? It could have solved another problem for you.'

'Who do you think it was attacked you? The alley tomcat?'

The pause I allowed was not purely for effect. Andy's touch was masterly, but I needed time to adapt to the new dimension he had introduced. 'I don't get it. I thought—'

'You assumed I was there as back-up. Sorry, Rodgers, to disenchant you. Didn't you twig? The occasion was tailor-made for giving you a jolt. So I did.'

'What was the point, for God's sake?'

'Ah—well. At that time, you see, I still had hopes of you. Give him a chance, I thought. With the Governor out of the way, maybe he'll assert himself, take the *Planet* down a new track, clean it up. Especially if he's given a taste of what it's like to be on the receiving end of this sick society that people like him have helped create. Maybe he'll see reason. Maybe . . . But it was futile. Straight afterwards, what was the first thing you did? Went ahead with full coverage of that Backstage filth, involving your own offspring. More than that— you hurried along to watch, and you even dragged me with you. I saw you then, Rodgers, for what you really are. Beyond redemption. Now do you understand?'

Utter silence crawled back into the car.

It was Elaine's voice that drove it out again. 'Please, Andy, let them go.' The tone had an ingratiating quality that I had never before heard from her, even when she was a child. 'I'll do anything you want. You've only got to say.'

'I wish you wouldn't talk like that.'

The note of sadness inherent in the remark switched startlingly to one of shrill fury. '*Mr Kent!* That's my name, you little guttersnipe. Call me that when you speak to me. Is that clear?'

'Sorry . . . I'm sorry. I didn't think . . .'

On screen, Elaine's contribution would have earned her an Oscar on the verbal evidence alone. One part of me was standing back to admire; the remainder was in a state of blue funk. Still no vestige of a reaction from the hunched figure at my side, six inches away. How far did we have to go?

'Of course you didn't *think*. When did girls of your age ever pause to consider? You hadn't a thought in your head when you walked out. You haven't now.'

'I don't understand. Please, Mr Kent, I don't know what—'

'No need to act the innocent with me, my girl. You know what I'm talking about.'

'Really, I don't. I wish you'd explain . . .'

'Explain?' The word darted like a whiplash. 'Who owes who an explanation? Didn't you have a decent upbringing? Every help and guidance? Don't try to deny it. Your mother and I . . .'

Andy's voice tailed off on a choke. The realism was almost too much to bear. Presently, more calmly, he restarted. 'We did all we humanly could to set you on the right path. What thanks did I get? When it came to the crunch, you knew best. Oh yes. The high life. That's what you were after: that's what you were determined to chase and find. Did you find it, Jilly? Did you?'

'You're confusing me with someone else. I've never—'

'Don't you tell *me* I'm confused.'

A vibrant hush. After a few moments Andy resumed in a

voice that had softened to verge upon the maudlin. 'I didn't mean to shout at you, Jilly. You know that. Don't take it to heart.'

'I'm not Jilly, Mr Kent. I'm Elaine Rodgers. I'm an actress who—'

'Ah, they all change their names. First thing they do. The ritual snapping of the family ties. But they don't sever, you know. Not completely. They cling on by a thread. So there's never any peace. You have to keep on, keep trying to repair the damage. That's all I've been doing.'

'Damage?'

'Some way to go yet. The list gets longer all the time. But it's so worthwhile. Cleansing the world of its stains—isn't that an end worth achieving? Repeat this, Jilly, after me. *O Lord, grant us strength and resolve to fulfil our holy task, to undertake all such—*'

'I tell you, I'm no relation of yours. Why won't you listen?'

When Andy spoke again, his voice had reverted to normal. 'You two in front. Get out of the car.'

After an interval I said stupidly, 'Now?'

'I want you to do it slowly and carefully. No sudden movements. When you're out, I want you both to walk over to that tree—the one straight ahead of us—and stand side by side with your backs against it. Understood?'

'If we do that—'

'Switch on the headlamps first.'

'Just one moment.'

In the act of reaching for the switch, I froze.

The command had come from Maxwell. There was no bluster behind it. His voice was cool, clear, packed with the kind of authority that evoked theatre footlights, last-night oratory. The pause that followed reinforced the impression of a measured approach, a considered response to a situation alive with possibilities. My heart sank. We were dealing not merely with formidable strength and guile, but intellect.

Andy seemed to have sensed it too. He was waiting.

'If we refuse to get out,' continued Maxwell, 'as we undoubtedly shall . . . would you mind informing us what you propose to do about it?'

'I'm the one holding the knife—or had you forgotten? Unless you—'

'You know, this scheme of yours doesn't strike me as having been properly thought out. Or else it's under-rehearsed. If I were in charge of it as a stage presentation, I'd be adapting and re-shaping as I went along.'

'Talk like that won't get you anywhere.' Andy sounded less assured. I hoped he had ideas about how to proceed. I had none, myself. 'What do you take me for, a frustrated producer? You can't teach me anything about flexibility. Ask your pal Rodgers. He'll tell you—'

'That tree, for example. The one you want us to stand by. Have you done your homework on it?'

'What are you blathering about?'

'From here, you can just make out the width of the trunk. But do you see what I do? Take a good, hard look. See what I'm getting at?'

'It's pitch-black, you ugly cretin. Unless you've infra-red vision—'

'Exactly.' Maxwell sounded as if he were winding up a debate. 'I suggest you look between the seats, straight ahead. Now do you see? A shade to the right, just under the lowest bough, the one with the . . .'

'Watch it, Andy,' I snapped.

I was too late. Between the seat-backs something had shot rearwards: out of the darkness came a hiss, then a yelp of pain. This was pursued by a moment of hiatus before Maxwell's voice resumed composedly, as if there had been no interruption. 'Slide clear, Elaine. It's all right.'

'You're sure?'

'I've got him.'

'Elaine,' I said urgently. 'Don't—'

Again I was behind events. The nearside rear door opened and slammed. From Andy I could hear a series of muffled groans. Helpless, bereft of counter-measures, I sat awaiting developments. They came without delay.

'Mr Rodgers. Would you mind please doing exactly as I say? Switch on all the lights you've got, then follow your daughter out of the car.'

'Andy?' Humiliatingly, my voice shook. 'Should I do what he wants?'

'Get the hell out of it!'

The roar came from Maxwell. So did the follow-up shove that pitched me violently against the offside door, sending a lance of agony through my neck and shoulder. With my left hand I fumbled for the catch, released it, felt the door yield and fly outwards. I was still held by the seat-belt. Stabbing downwards, I disengaged the mechanism.

I was outside, grovelling in leaf-mould. Suddenly the encircling trees were lit up. Elaine came into view: half-sprawled across the offside wing of the car, she was weeping hysterically. At my touch she let out a shriek, tried to squirm free. For a moment we struggled: then I slapped her, fiercely.

'Elaine! It's me. Get a grip on yourself.'

Half-collapsing against my chest, she went on sobbing uncontrollably. As well as keeping her upright, I was trying to peer round to see what was happening inside the car. The light from the headlamps was no help: the Cavalier's interior remained in gloom. I could hear nothing. Only Elaine's hiccuping distress, and then her efforts to talk.

'The knife . . . Has Jimmy got the knife?'

'There's no knife, Elaine. Don't you remember? You and Andy—'

A rear door of the car flew open. There was an eruption, a thud, a yell. Out of the shadows a figure was coming at us. Elaine screamed.

I turned to grapple with the onrush. An arm was held high, elevating something that glinted in the glare. Aimlessly, with a foot, I kicked out. I missed, but miraculously the figure lurched to a halt, wavered, was dragged back.

With a protective arm about Elaine I bawled, 'Did you get him, Andy?'

A sound reached me that suggested flesh hitting flesh.

Presently, from behind the open car door appeared a shape, brushing itself down. It seemed to be cursing to itself. Elaine let out a tearful laugh, one of purest relief. 'Jimmy? You're okay? You fixed him?'

'For God's sake!' I was trying to haul her to the other side of the car, away from the shambling outline as it approached. Her resistance thwarted me. 'You don't understand!' I yelled into her ear. 'He's the one we have to avoid. He's the man who—'

'On the contrary, Peter.' The misshapen director had come to a standstill two yards from us. He seemed to be examining the ground. Abruptly he crouched, picked up something, eyed it for an instant, dropped it rattlingly upon the bonnet of the car. 'We'd better take that along,' he said calmly. 'It'll be needed as evidence.' He threw me another glance. 'As I was about to say, you're the one who doesn't understand. The villain's in the back seat, out cold. Might I suggest we all get back in and drive to the nearest police station?' He made a self-mocking noise in his throat. 'Not much of a curtain-line, but it'll have to do.'

CHAPTER 22

Theatre crush-bars never were designed for coherent conversation. Leaving Laura to study the wall-photos of scenes from past hits, I battled into position for securing a couple of drinks within a time-scale that would afford us a minimum of ninety seconds to get them down. Happily, someone of large build moved out of my path at a vital moment, letting me through.

When I got back, Laura was standing with her hands folded demurely in front of her, watching with absorption the writhing profiles of the couple exchanging views nearest to her left flank. I pressed a glass into her palm.

'Picking up ideas for the page?'

'God forbid. I'm here to relax.'

'Having any luck?'

'It's demanding work,' she admitted. 'You need to stick at it.'

'If you'll forgive a corny question . . . what do you think of the play?'

Her nose wrinkled. 'Just tell me one thing. Did Elaine have trouble learning her lines?'

'No, neither of them gave her the slightest bother.'

'In a wild sort of way, I'm not un-enjoying it. Elaine doesn't have to open her mouth. She's a sensation. Monday's centre-spread hardly did her justice.'

'The *Planet* always did have a tendency to underplay things.'

'But you'll be putting that right, I expect.' Laura peeped at me from behind her glass. 'Is Katie here, do you know?'

'If she is, she's keeping out of sight.' My essay at indifference was less than a success. 'Probably she couldn't make it. Her agent—'

'I think someone's trying to attract your attention.'

Following her gaze, I turned. Katie, clad in green and beige satin, was standing silently behind me, holding a glass of something colourless with a slice of lemon drifting on its surface. She gave me an attentive inspection, then nodded.

'Yep. It's indubitably the celebrated Mr Peter Rodgers of E.C.4., tracker of villains, fearless exposer of The Truth.

Does he have time, I wonder, for an off-diary interview?'

I made a show of consulting my watch. 'Only with friends or near relatives.'

'In that case . . .' Her mouth stretched into a lopsided smile. I couldn't hold back an answering grin. Then I kissed her: after that we went into a bear-hug routine. Somebody took a flashlight picture. 'That,' Laura said dispassionately from the sidelines, 'will emerge as a smudge in tomorrow's *Record*. Who cares?'

'Listen,' I told Katie. 'I want to—'

She planted a finger across my lips. 'No repentant verbiage—okay? From either side.'

'It's a deal.'

'Well,' she asked, 'what do you make of Elaine and her latest vehicle?'

'What do *you* make of it?'

'My third novel, actually. It's given me a great idea, which might just work. Remind me to thank Elaine after the performance. Though I still think,' she added, giving the slice of lemon a swirl, 'she's abusing her talents. Remind me to mention that, too.'

'Remind me,' I requested Laura, 'to forget to remind her. Katie, I don't believe you've met Laura Cadey, our Women's Woman. Another fan of Elaine's. I think.'

Katie surveyed her with attention. 'Saw your byline, back in the week. The background to the Andy Kent story.'

Laura flinched. 'That was a special feature I'd have been happier without. But somehow I . . .'

'You didn't want it done by anyone else,' I supplied.

Katie nodded comprehendingly. 'His wife was a friend of yours?'

'They were both friends of mine.' Laura glanced away.

On a note of practical diversion Katie said, 'The part about the typewriter interested me.'

'Sheer chance,' I explained. 'That Laski portable seemed

hell-bent on throwing suspicion upon Jimmy Maxwell, but in fact it was just in the routine course of events that it found its way via the girl temp to a firm of theatrical costumiers that Maxwell happens to patronize. It does appear that he could conceivably have made use of the machine, on the sly, during his visits to the showroom . . . but of course he didn't. Before getting rid of it, Andy Kent had already used it to type out a couple of the Censor letters—including the one to me.'

'So it was all planned well ahead?'

'He had a selection of notes waiting in the pipeline, all set for delivery as required. The list was quite extensive.'

'Was every note typed on the Laski?'

'No. He used a variety of machines. He'd plenty to choose from, both at the agency when he was there, and at Planet House when he moved to us.'

'Why did he move? What was the point?'

'His purpose,' I said slowly, 'was to get himself nicely into position to tackle Sir Giles . . . whom he chiefly blamed for what had become of his daughter Jilly.'

'Ah. The talent contest. But that was your baby as well, surely?'

'Yes, but he seemed to have this idea that I might have been persuaded to run it against my better judgement. So he went for the Governor first, to see how I'd react. Apparently I disappointed him.'

'He certainly was a nut.' Kate pondered. 'Only a lunatic,' she added, 'could have gone to the length of actually drawing your attention to the fact that he'd owned a Laski himself. It was inviting trouble.'

'Not to that extent. He knew that he'd be the one sent off to make inquiries about it. Besides, by that time I don't think he gave a damn. He'd become arrogant—a man with a self-appointed mission to fumigate society—and I doubt if it entered his head that anything like that could rebound on him. He probably enjoyed dropping hints. Looking back, I can recall quite a number.' I shook my head. 'I must have been deaf and blind.'

'No more than the rest of us.' Laura dumped her Campari on a convenient ledge, as though she had lost the taste for it.

'No one,' Katie pointed out, 'could possibly have known. The ruination of his daughter was hardly in the public eye, was it? What exactly did happen to her, after she won the contest?'

'One imagines it turned her head.' I consulted Laura, who nodded.

'She did have talent,' she said bleakly. 'What she lacked was the character to go with it. Or maybe she just got into the wrong hands. I wouldn't know. The fact is, inside a year she was well hooked into the drug scene and all that it involved. Her showbiz career faded out. What a waste!' Grabbing the Campari back, she took an abstracted gulp.

'Where is she now?' asked Katie.

'Locked in a rather small room inside a special institution, refusing to answer questions from a headshrink.'

'My God. Is there any hope for her?'

I shrugged. 'You'd better ask her psychiatrist.' I wanted to leave the topic but Katie was persistent, her novelist's curiosity aroused.

'This accounts, then, for her father's obsession with anybody in the world of entertainment? Quite apart from yourself, he regarded them all as responsible for what had happened to his Jilly?'

'I don't know about *all*. But anyone whose work he saw as salacious, mind-twisting—yes, undoubtedly. According to the official theory, it was enough to convince him that it was his sacred duty to weed them out, purify the soil.'

'A debt he owed to his wife,' added Laura. 'We all thought her death was accidental, but there's a query over that now. Her mind could have been blown by Jilly's disaster. She might have steered deliberately into that tree.'

'How awful.' Katie gazed unseeingly across the bar.

Laura smiled at her. 'I can see book-titles revolving in your head. *The Culprits. The Mind Manipulators.* You can have those on the house.'

'Thanks.' Katie turned her gaze upon me. 'You don't think there's any chance that Elaine . . . ?'

'Your sister,' I reassured her, 'is much too down-to-earth for that. Apart from which, she has her Jimmy to keep her on course. I've had to revise my ideas about him,' I said ruefully.

'Don't fret about it, Dad. We all make mistakes.'

The house buzzer transmitted its third summons and there was a general drift away from the bar. Swallowing the last of her drink, Katie crossed herself. 'Stand by,' she remarked, 'for another hour of eloquent silence, broken by pauses. You know who should have the main credit for this production? The dog-trainer. He did a great job.'

'Can you look in some time,' asked Laura, 'for a chat? I'd like to do a piece on the new book.'

'As long as it's you inviting me,' said Katie, with a dark glance in my direction.

'No collusion,' Laura promised.

She held me back for a moment as Katie started moving with the tide. 'One day, Peter, you will tell me, won't you?'

'Tell you?'

'The full story. Everything that took place inside the car in Epping Forest.'

'You can have it right now,' I replied. 'I discovered two things: Elaine doesn't spend her entire life acting, and I'm not half as astute as I thought I was.'

Laura's hand gave mine a squeeze as we joined the slow ebb from the bar. 'Speaking personally,' she murmured, 'I still think you're quite brainy. Two gifted daughters can't spring from nowhere. I wonder if . . .'

'No harm,' I observed, as she paused, 'in putting it to the test. Are you going to tell them, or shall I?'

'In my opinion,' she said thoughtfully, 'it's Daddy's job. Stepmothers-to-be have enough on their plates, thank you, without that.'